The Captive

A Story of Fear & Forgiveness

Jeannie G Bruenning

Prologue

Abaddon sat at the far end of the table in an attempt to keep as much distance from Patho as possible. Patho had become hideous to look at, barely resembling his former self. To Abaddon's perturbation his own appearance had also begun to change. He added it to the ever-growing list of effects and results from choosing to follow Patho. The extended time in the Pit, which had recently been forced upon him, was taking its toll. Abaddon couldn't understand how Serpent could come and go as he pleased. This angered Patho immensely, but from Abaddon's vantage point, Patho was unable to control him. The friction between the two was more than Abaddon could, or wanted to, tolerate.

"What are you suggesting?" Secretary asked in his annoying high-pitched screeching tone.

Abaddon cringed every time he spoke. He much preferred Patho's first assistant, at least Abaddon could read him. But since his untimely and unexplainable disappearance, Abaddon was now forced to deal with Secretary. In his experience, the only difference between Secretary and Serpent was that Patho still had a little control over him. From where Abaddon stood, Secretary was as bad, evil and annoying as Serpent. In the past, these were traits that typically drew such characters to Abaddon. But he was becoming increasingly tiresome of these three using him as their whipping boy.

Serpent hissed in long-drawn-out phrases, "He wantss you to make the Fallen Souls ssso fearful, they stop making requestsss for redemption. You're not as bright asss the lassst one, are you?"

Secretary glared at Serpent. He may not be as bright, but he was certainly more daring.

"I not only want them to stop, I want them to revoke their original request!" Patho sneered with teeth grinding. His eyes were squinted, and his jaw locked as he said slowly and defined, "I DON'T CARE WHAT IT TAKES! The hair on Abaddon's neck stood up. "If I am told of one more Fallen Soul seeking forgiveness," Patho clenched his fist so tightly the bones cracked. He stretched his head as far to one side as it would go, "...there will be consequences." Patho's entire being began to twitch.

"We don't know how they make requests," Abaddon said.

"THEN FIND OUT!" Patho sneered.

"I suggest that we recruit assistance," offered Secretary.

"You mean from the Fallen Souls? The Fallen Souls will never assist us," Abaddon said.

"Oooh, there are some that will," Serpent said with a hint of excitement, which was all the excitement he could muster. He tilted

to one side from his crouched position on the ground. He put his hands together and began tapping his fingers in controlled rhythm.

"Who?" Abaddon asked sharply.

"Ahhh…those who have returned to the darkness," Secretary offered as he looked at Serpent. "Don't you agree?"

This time he had Serpent's approval. "Yesssss," Serpent replied with evil mischief in his voice, "Those who have returned to the darkness." He began to roll his hands as if in preparation for a meal.

Abaddon huffed and shook his head, "The ones I've seen are lifeless, almost comatose," he said.

"Not all of them!" Serpent said with great pleasure. "There are some whose anger and hatred erupts continuously at the mention," he paused and slowly and intentionally turned toward Patho, "THE KING."

As expected, Patho shook at his name. Serpent was entertained by Patho's reactions and had perfected his timing when he spoke. "They are angry and bitter — just the right combination for this little task."

"Angry and bitter," said Secretary, "music to my ears."

"This is no little task," Abaddon argued.

The room fell silent. Secretary looked down and began making notes. Serpent remained crouched in the layer of filth that covered the Pit, only his eyes moved. He looked from side to side suspiciously and with anticipation.

Unable to endure any length of silence, Patho abruptly shouted, "What are you waiting for? Did I not make myself clear? I WANT THE REQUESTS FOR FORGIVENESS TO END NOW!!!"

To the Fallen Souls who have not realized the need for forgiveness,
May your journey lead you back to the King.

1

The King turned the page with great care and continued reading. Balbas sat nervously watching. There wasn't an inch of him that didn't want to jump up from the table, bolt through the doors and head back to the lower chambers.

Whatever made me think I could do this? he thought. *Write what you know, they always say. Write what you know.*

Konnory watched from across the table. He could sense Balbas' angst. He could also feel the nervous vibration of his uncontrollable bouncing knee. The King had this effect on those who came into his presence. It wasn't of his doing, it was the result of the guests' own insecurity. Those who entered his presence humbly, immediately felt his love. Those who entered fearfully had to face their own demons before accepting his grace.

The King turned the page.

Balbas began quietly tapping his hand on the table. *Why did I let him talk me into this?* He looked up at Konnory who responded with a smile. *I should have never told anyone, especially Konnory. Whatever made me think I could pull it off?* Balbas glanced at the door. *There is no one in my way. If I were to make a run for it, I would have to keep going. If I leave now, I could never return to the lower chambers.*

Konnory observed his every move. *He has it bad,* he thought. *Maybe this was not the best idea. I thought he was ready. He may have needed more time.*

The King sighed, making both turn their attention his way.

He doesn't like it, I knew it. Konnory, why did you make me do this? I said no! Didn't I say no? Why didn't I stand up to you? "No, I don't want the King to read this." That's all it would have taken; two little letters that would have stopped this catastrophe from happening. No! No no no no no no no no no. He looked up at Konnory with all the resentment he could muster. His eyes tightened.

"It's OK," Konnory mouthed.

The King turned another page.

This is torture. I can't write! This was a great idea in the beginning. Record the events of Turayn as told by those watching and protecting its inhabitants. Keep a record that can be passed on until the last Fallen Soul returns. They need to remember — or maybe they don't. Maybe once in the Kingdom, we are to forget it all. What made me think that he hadn't already thought of this? Surely, he has assigned someone to document the history of Turayn. Surely, it is being documented somewhere. Balbas glanced once again at Konnory, who nodded his head ever so gently, and the King turned another page.

He's almost to the end. It's almost over. What will I say when he tells me I should not have attempted such a feat? I'm going to lose my position. He won't let me back in the lower chambers. I wouldn't let me back, why would he?

Balbas was too focused on creating an escape route to notice the misty glance from the King. Konnory saw it. He knew where the King must be in his reading. The King's eyes fell back on the pages of the large book he held in his hands.

He's reading of Jael and those final hours, Konnory thought as he took a deep breath.

The King turned the page and wiped the tear that softly rolled down his cheek.

Konnory looked back at Balbas, whose attention seemed to be elsewhere. He wanted to stand up and shout, "You're missing it!! Get out of your head and take notice of what is happening right here!"

It's as I expected, Father loves it, Konnory thought. *How could He not? It's a record of the Fallen Souls. None of us could have ever written it in such a way. I can't imagine the time Balbas has invested in this. The conversations with the Watchers, the stories he has heard. Balbas, you are missing it.*

The King turned the page.

Konnory understood the gentle smile that began to illuminate Father. He kicked Balbas under the table. Balbas stiffened. Konnory motioned for him to look at the King.

Balbas clenched his jaw. He stiffened further. *This was not for the King's eyes,* he shouted in his head. *This was for my children. No, I don't have children, but I may someday. I didn't want them to forget. I never want them to forget. Even after the last Fallen Soul is in the Kingdom, I don't want them to forget. What made me think I could write the creation of Turayn? Of homecomings such as Waldemar, Taytan and Odella? Odella, what will she think of this? She should have been the one to write it. She would have done it beautifully. She could have spoken first hand of ruling in Turayn, or Konnory, for that matter. He could have written it. Perhaps he has, and this is just a ploy to get rid of me.* Balbas glared at Konnory. *Konnory, why didn't you write this? It's not that brilliant of an idea - after all, I thought of it. Carasi, he should have done it. He was there all along. Planning and watching every move. I am so unworthy. Crazy! Crazy, crazy, crazy....*

Balbas was so preoccupied with the conversation in his head that he failed to hear the King close the book. Konnory kicked him again. Balbas stiffened. His lips were clenched tightly. He glared across the table.

The King took a breath and Balbas froze. "It's beautiful," the King whispered.

"I knew you would like it," Konnory said.

"What are you calling it?" the King asked.

Calling it? Wait! What! What did I miss? Is he addressing me? He couldn't be...

"Balbas," the King said softy. "When you are finished with your private conversation, I would like to talk to you about this book." Balbas turned his head slowly. "It's beautifully written. What gave you the idea?"

"Sire, I'm at a loss for words," Balbas finally replied.

"I don't believe that," the King said as he patted the book.

There was silence, a long silence. "Perhaps he is at a loss," Konnory said.

Balbas sat back slightly in his chair. He took a deep breath, and then another. "I only wanted to create a record, something that would never allow us to forget."

"And what made you think of using the stories from the Watchers rather than the documentation that is being kept?" asked the King.

"Because they were there," Balbas replied shrugging his shoulders, "they are there,"

"Yes, they are," the King responded nodding his head.

"They were there not as Fallen Souls, but they were here, watching the day of the fall. They were with you when you spoke Turayn into being. On the day you and the Princes journeyed for the first time to Turayn. They watched as you walked Waldemar back to the Kingdom. They assisted Latzof in building the boat and watched in amazement as you called all the creatures of Turayn to come. When Odella took the throne as King Haddad, they were there."

The King and Konnory watched Balbas as the words rolled off his tongue. These were no longer just stories to him. He spoke as if he, too, had been there.

Balbas instantly transformed from a mounting bundle of nervous energy to a confident, well-spoken representative. His leg no longer shaking under the table, his hands folded softly in front of him. He continued, "When they spoke of Jael's entry into Turayn, it was always with great care. Telling of how they watched the Son of the King become human, causes most of them to break.

"They recall the day Jael saw them clearly for the first time, the relief that they could now communicate with him. They laugh as they tell of Magnor's tree incidents," he paused.

"They love to tell of the humans reaction to Jael's Works of the Kingdom; the day he healed that brave woman and brought the child back to life. Their stories are never about Jael, but about the reactions of the crowd, or the one being healed. It always makes them laugh." Balbas began to laugh.

"Listening to Watchers talk of the Humans is one thing, hearing them actually laugh - is quite another."

"I'm not sure I knew they could laugh," Konnory said.

"Oh, yes. It's like nothing you've ever heard," Balbas continued.

"Yes, and you are right, it is a rapturous sound," the King replied.

"They weren't laughing when they talked of Jael and Quaine's reunion. No, there wasn't a dry eye then. It must have been an amazing sight. I wish I could have witnessed it," Balbas said.

"You wrote as if you did," the King offered.

"Thank you, Sire," Balbas said bowing his head. Balbas was having a difficult time breathing. There seemed so much breath in him, he may pass out. "Your acknowledgment means the world to me." The room was quiet once again.

"You've recorded recent events, very recent in fact," the King said.

"Yes, Sire. There isn't a day that goes by when I don't add to it," Balbas said. "But I believe its complete now. Jael is home."

"What of the last chapter? When will you tell of Jael's homecoming?" asked the King.

Beads of perspiration beginning to form on his brow, Konnory could once again feel the rhythm of his knee. "No, Sire, I couldn't write of Jael's homecoming. I could never do it justice."

"You are mistaken," replied the King. Balbas' mouth opened in preparation for a rebuttal before he remembered to whom he was addressing. "You owe me one last chapter." Konnory caught a glimpse of an all too familiar smirk from the King. "I will expect it in three days."

"Those would be Turayn days," Konnory quickly added. Balbas looked up at the King for confirmation. He did not receive one.

"Three days," said the King.

"Three days, then this is over," Balbas said ever so quietly.

"Over?" Konnory burst out. "It's just beginning my friend! You and I have much to do." Instantly, Balbas moved from concern to very concerned.

"We?" he asked.

"Yes, my friend - WE!"

"You've not filled him in?" asked the King.

"Not yet. I was waiting for the right time. I guess it's now," Konnory replied. "You have been selected to assist me. We know that there is going to be those who are committed to eliminating Jael's teachings in Turayn. If they have it their way, this will include anyone who follows his teachings."

"Am I to accompany you?" Balbas asked with reluctant excitement.

"No," replied Konnory, "At least not at this time. You will remain here, doing everything you do already. The only difference is that you will be focused on a select group of humans." Balbas never took his eyes off Konnory. "You will be collecting information, organizing the Watchers, and keeping an accurate accounting of each operation."

"This we now know you can do quite well," the King offered.

Balbas smiled, grateful for the compliment. "Who will be the focus of our efforts?"

"You, my friend, are going to be focused on those who have such hatred for the King and Jael, that they dedicate their lives to eradicating it."

"That will indeed be a challenge," Balbas said. "When will this begin? Do you have someone in mind already?"

"Konnory will be accompanying Jael to Turayn for his final visit," the King replied.

"Jael is returning?" Balbas interrupted.

"He is," said the King. "He is eager to return. Your new assignment begins now. The Watchers are already on the lookout for those who need our special attention."

"They will be reporting back to you," Konnory continued, "and we will be coming up with our game plan."

"Is there anyone they are currently watching?" Balbas asked.

"Yes, in fact, there is," Konnory replied. "He is evil. If I didn't know better, I would think he was Patho. The Watchers will fill you in, they have kept a close eye on him for a while now." Konnory paused, looking directly at Balbas, "Are you sure you are up for this assignment?"

Balbas response was not immediate. He looked at Konnory and then to the King. He dropped his head for a moment, considering the obligation he would be making. "Without a doubt," he replied.

"Glad to hear it!" said the King.

"Then it is time to begin," Konnory said. "You have some work to do and I have a brother who is eager to begin a trip."

The three left the Throne Room and walked silently down the hall; there was far too many thoughts bombarding Balbas' mind to carry on any conversation. As they approached the Dining Room, Konnory and the King stopped. The stood watch while Balbas continued on.

"He's going to make a great comrade for you," the King said.

Konnory nodded. "I'll have my very own Waldemar," he replied.

"The record that he wrote, I'm curious, what does he call it?" asked the King.

Konnory reached to open the Dining Room door, "The Plan," he replied.

2

The King and Konnory's entrance into the Dining Room in no way interrupted the conversation.

"What?" asked Odella, "What visit?"

Magnor reached over and took her hand. With a gentle nod, he calmed her. Odella had participated more frequently in family gatherings since Jael's return. She had been reluctant at first; it took coaxing from both the King and Queen to reassure her that her place would always be next to Magnor.

Magnor had not required the same degree of assurance. He had made peace with the fact that Odella had left. He was at peace with the fact that she had changed. She was not the confident person he had fallen in love with, but what she may be lacking in confidence was replaced with a new depth of wisdom. He would have her no other place than by his side.

"Yes, Odella," Jael replied. "They need to know it isn't over. They need to see me. To be honest, I want to see them. I won't stay long, I promise." Jael was looking directly at Odella, but he was far away. Although this quieted her, she was not calm.

13

Konnory walked over to her and stood with his arms held out as if he were a trophy. "I'm going with him!" he said with great pride and delight. It was just enough humor to brake the tension.

"Is that supposed to make me feel better?" she responded.

"Do you think I shouldn't go?" Konnory asked, very dejected. Odella shook her head. She knew very well it would be a waste of time and energy to argue.

Quietly, as if in a whisper, Quaine asked, "Why would you want to go back?" As quiet as it was spoken, it was heard in great volume.

Konnory dropped his shoulders from the weight of the question. "Why wouldn't we?" he asked.

Quaine didn't respond as he sat with his head lowered.

Carasi pushed back his chair; the scratching of the chair legs against the ground drew everyone's attention from Quaine. "When are you leaving?" he asked.

"The sooner the better," Jael replied. "Do you have any instructions?"

"No! You are on your own for this one!" Carasi responded. "Besides, you are the only one who would know what to expect."

Konnory now stood behind Jael's chair, and grabbing it with his hands, he said, "Let's get on our way."

"Anxious, are we?" Jael asked.

"Yes, as a matter of fact," Konnory replied.

"You've been very patient," Father said reassuringly. "You know it isn't the same from the first time you were there?"

"That's one of the reasons why I'm so excited. To be able to see those changes, to remember what it was like from the beginning."

"You may be able to answer some of my questions," Jael said.

"Don't I always," Konnory jest.

"Enough," said the King, "if you have to go, then off with both of you." Jael stood, grabbed Konnory's sleeve, and headed for the door. As the two exited, the King grinned, "both of them in Turayn..."

Jael and Konnory were escorted back to Turayn by a small regiment of Watchers. Jael did not rush the journey. With every step, he relived his last few days there. Konnory sensed his brother's emotion. Those accompanying Jael formed a protective circle around him.

As this small group of travelers entered Turayn, they were greeted by a dozen or so additional Watchers. Their acknowledgment of Jael was warm and heartfelt. This group was present when Jael entered Turayn as an infant. They had been there when he and his human brothers had played by the sea. They were there the day Patho met him in the desert. It was after that meeting that they had made themselves visible to Jael for the first time. They watched his every move, his every step. They watched as he was arrested and beaten; knowing that they were unable to protect or assist without his asking. Now, this group welcomed him back, no longer a Human but the Son of the King.

The Watchers had not left Jael's followers since he left. It had been difficult to watch their suffering and sorrow, unable to comfort them, unable to tell them if Jael would return or not.

"There remains a small group gathered outside the place where you entered the Pit." they informed him.

"Are they the first on our agenda?" Konnory asked.

"Yes," replied Jael, "but we will be the Watchers this time." Jael turned to the group, "Make yourselves known to them. Tell them to return home, I will be there shortly."

With those instructions, the Watchers, Konnory, and Jael made their way to the site where they found four women waiting. Jael could feel their fear and confusion. They were no longer the strong, independent women who walked with him just a short time ago. They were weak, brittle beings.

Jael resisted the urge to reach out and comfort them. The shock of seeing him may have been too much for them. Two Watchers slowly and ever so carefully made themselves visible.

"Do not be afraid," one said.

Jael sighed, *'Do not be afraid.' How many times did I say those words? Those four words were the beginning of every visit a Watcher ever made.*

Do not be afraid, Jael said to himself. "It won't be until they return to the Kingdom that they will be able to obey that command," he said quietly to Konnory. Konnory nodded.

The voice startled the women, grabbing and holding on to each other for comfort and security. The Watchers spoke as Jael had instructed. With each word, the women began to feel a spark of assurance that quickly quenched their fears.

"Return and tell the others that he will see them shortly," the Watchers instructed.

The women slowly stood, taking time to regain their balance. In a few moments the news began burning within them. The journey back home began with slow, calculated steps. With each step, there seemed to be added anticipation, added excitement.

The women made their way to the home of Gad, which had become a refuge for Jael's close followers. The home had been filled with great sorrow, the sorrow that darkens a room while sucking the life out of it. The conversation was woven with regrets, questions, and at times, anger.

What had they missed? Why did this happen? He was their hope; why did it come to an end so quickly?

The women burst through the door. "He's not dead!" one of them blurted out.

"They said he is alive!" said another.

Life came back to those in attendance at the same time confusion and disbelief entered the room. The women had the groups' full attention as they entered the home.

"What nonsense are you speaking?" Gad demanded.

"Get them something to drink, they've gone mad," Thomas ordered.

"No! We are not mad, it happened - it really happened!" the women insisted. "They said that Jael is alive."

"Who said?" asked Gad.

"Them," one of the women replied as she pointed in the direction of the tomb.

"Who's them? The guards?" questioned Gad.

"NO!" Mary said very insistently. "Listen to me! Two men were there, they said that Jael was – or is - alive. They said not to be afraid."

Gad grabbed James' arm and both darted out the door. Running as fast as they could, weaving through the crowded streets until they reached the tomb. James arrived first with Gad on his heels. The two entered, and stopped abruptly. Lying where Jael had been placed were the clothes that had wrapped his disfigured body. The other followers arrived shortly and crowded around the entrance.

"Is he in there?" someone shouted.

Gad and James slowly exited, bewildered. "No, no he is not," replied Gad.

Mary was the only one to remain in the home. She walked out to a small courtyard just behind the house. She stood gazing up into the sky. There she stood in silence repeating what the Watchers had said. She wanted to remember their words. She wanted to believe their message.

"Where are the others?"

Neither the question nor the voice startled her. Mary assumed it was a fellow follower who had just arrived. "They went to see for themselves," Mary responded without turning around.

"They did not believe you?"

Mary smiled. Still gazing up, "No, they did not. Gad thought we were mad."

"Do you believe?"

"I want to," Mary answered. "With everything that is within me, I want to."

There was a moment's pause, and then she heard her name, "Mary."

She froze, afraid to turn around, afraid not to. She knew that voice. But if she turned and it wasn't him.... She couldn't stop herself, she slowly turned and as her eyes fell upon him, she sank to her knees. "Jael" she said softly.

Jael walked over to her and knelt down. Taking her hands in his, he softly replied, "Yes, it is I."

Mary began to weep. "You were ... gone," she whispered.

"Don't be afraid, Mary," he said ever so gently. "I had to go." Mary began to sob. Jael placed his hand on her shoulder to comfort her. "You've heard and now you have seen. Tell Gad you are not mad; that you have seen me, and I am alive." Jael wiped her tears. It seemed impossible for her to regain her composure.

"You said," she forced out each word, "You said you had to go, but..." Dropping her head again, she sobbed uncontrollably, as the grief and pain she had lived with these past few days began to release their grip.

Jael knelt patiently. "It's alright," he whispered. Again, he waited.

"What they put you through," Mary finally whispered. "And there was nothing we could do..."

"There was nothing you needed to do," Jael said. "There was nothing for you to do."

She gazed up at him. She took his hand and held it in hers. As she rubbed his palm, she felt it. She looked down, the marks still remained. It caught her off guard. Her head jerked away, unable to see anymore. She eventually found the strength to look up into his eyes.

He smiled gently. "Those will remain. It will be a reminder to all," he said.

They sat in silence for a bit longer. When he felt she was once again strong enough to stand, Jael helped her to her feet. "Tell them that I will visit them all soon." Jael gently squeezed her hands and said once again, "Don't be afraid, Mary."

Mary stood looking up into Jael's face. There were no words for her to speak. Standing in front of her was the one who had changed her life. The man she had thought would be there always; the one she watched being beaten and put to death. The man she thought was gone forever.

"Tell the others," Jael said once again. Jael tightened his grip and then released Mary's hands. He turned and entered the home. There was only a second's hesitation before Mary started after him, but once she entered the house, he was nowhere to be found.

The front door burst open, startling her. Gad and James were once again the first to enter. They were discussing the possibilities of Jael's disappearance. As they entered the room where Mary stood, silence immediately fell. Gad walked over to her. He stared at her. There was something different in her expression. He could see that she had been crying, but she wasn't sad. The room was no longer darkened by sorrow, and Gad felt warm life in the air.

"What is it?" Gad asked.

"He was here," Mary softly replied. "He was here."

Gad's eyes widened. The others just stood there, not knowing what to do. Gad began to speak, but Mary held up her hand to stop him. "He said to tell you that I'm not mad." Gad smiled. "He said he would visit each one soon."

Mary looked at the group. She could understand their questioning. If she had been them, she would most likely not believe her own words. She turned and walked back out into the courtyard and again gazed up into the sky. The others quietly followed. They made a partial circle around her. Without prompting, Mary began to tell them of what she had just experienced. "He was here..." she began.

Later that day, Jael and Konnory were directed to a small group of men walking along the road. Jael immediately recognized each of the men. They were somber and heavy-hearted. Jael and Konnory approached the group from behind; it only took a few steps for the group to realize they had been joined by two strangers.

"May we join you?" Konnory asked.

There was no immediate response. Eventually, one looked at them in acknowledgment. As they walked, Jael recognized his surroundings. He knew this road. He and his followers had traveled it several times. Drawing his attention back to the group he said, "You seem troubled."

"We have lost a great teacher," one replied.

"I'm sorry for your loss," Jael said. "When did this happen?"

"Are you not aware that Jael was put to death? He was our leader."

"We are just arriving after a long absence, tell us what has happened," Konnory said.

The men began to explain the details of the last days. There were long, silent pauses between each recollection. They spoke of the last time they had eaten together, of Jael's arrest and unfair trial. No one was able to talk of his death. Konnory could see the pain in their eyes and the loss in their voices. He had known of every detail, but he was hearing it from those who had experienced it firsthand.

He was reminded of his own Garden experience when he had realized the separation between he and Father. He had known of those details as well, but experiencing it was something completely different. Knowing and experiencing are worlds apart. These men were feeling that kind of separation, but not with Father. Their separation was from Jael.

"This morning, it was reported that his body is missing."

"Who would have done such a thing?" another asked. "For a ransom! I am certain it will be used for a ransom!"

"A ransom from whom? We have nothing to pay as a ransom."

"We may not, but the Temple and Empire does. Perhaps the ones who took it think they would do anything to ensure that Jael's body remains secure."

They walked until they were entering a small town. Finding their way to the home where they had been invited to dine, they invited their guest to join them. Their grief filled the room. The meal was small, which equaled their appetites. As the bread was passed, Jael picked it up and as he had done so many times before with this group, he gave thanks and divided it.

It was at that moment that their eyes were open. There were gasps, tears, and shouts of joy. Konnory observed in laughter.

They flooded Jael with questions. He patiently answered each one. When it was time to depart, none of the men wanted to let Jael go.

"I will see you again. But we must leave you for today. Go and tell the others. I will see them all soon."

Jael and Konnory pulled themselves from the group and left the house. Once realizing they were gone, all ran to the door to call out to them, but their guests were nowhere to be seen. The group quickly made their exit and returned to the others. Their return took them a fraction of the time. Not only had their speed changed, their message had as well.

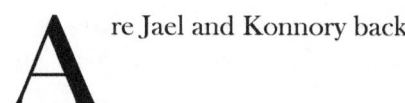

3

re Jael and Konnory back?"

"No, Father, they are still in Turayn. The reports say that they are doing well. I know it will be difficult for Jael to leave."

"Has Balbas left anything for Me?"

"Yes. He came in three times and then spun around and left. Finally, I inquired if he needed something. He showed me the papers and just stood there. I reached out to take them, and almost thought I wasn't going to get it out of his hands," said Ferrul

The King laughed. "Send someone to summons him back."

"That will surely calm his nerves," Ferrul said as he handed over the tablet. "Should he be told that you have made the request?"

"I think not. He may not come," replied the King.

With tablet in hand, the King settled in his chair next to the fireplace. The embers were still glowing from the morning's fire. He turned to the first page: *Jael's Return – The Final Chapter* was boldly written on page one.

The roar created from the rushing air was that of a great beast. They were an army in and of themselves. A multitude of warriors and chariots escorted Magnor and Jael as they returned to the Kingdom. Their presence illuminated the darkness. All the Kingdom awaited Jael's return, but no one's excitement and anticipation matched that of the King and Queen's.

As the processional approached the Kingdom, Magnor's chariot took a slight detour. Upon his command, this throng of warriors veered toward Turayn. Without turning around, Magnor leaned his head back and shouted, "They've earned the right to witness this homecoming!" Jael smiled. "We may not be able to bring them to the Kingdom for this celebration, but we'll give them what we can."

There was no hiding their approach. It was as if a galaxy of stars had spun free and was hurling through the atmosphere. The brilliant light and the roar drew the attention of each warrior. These who had guarded Turayn from without, felt the power of the approach. With great pride and excitement, they stood at attention as the royal procession passed by.

The Watchers also witnessed the triumphant exhibition. From every corner of Turayn, they began to shout in celebration. Their expression of victory could only be sensed by the

Humans, as the sounds were inaudible to the human ear. It translated as a distant thunder rolling across the universe. It was a Kingdomly sound. It filled the air in volumes and echoed back to the Kingdom.

Feeling as if they may actually burst, the Warriors felt the exhilaration of the return of their Prince and the admiration of the Watchers from within. This was a victory like no other. This was a celebration of those who had returned to the Kingdom, and renewed hope for the loved ones and friends that had not yet returned home.

From the outer regions of the Kingdom, cheers of celebration and welcome began to ring out upon seeing the chariots in the distance. As the chariots drew closer, the cheers spread throughout the land. The gates stood open in anticipation of the arrival. Those who had watched the flood of bodies leave on that day of Patho's deception could not help but compare that horrific departure to this victorious return.

Magnor took the King's chariot to the front gates of the castle where the King and Queen waited. Putting the reigns down, he turned to address Jael. He stood for a moment. He had watched Jael exit the Pit, he felt the exhilaration as his warriors stood at attention in honor of him, but he had not had the opportunity to welcome him. He had practiced his speech; he knew what he wanted to say. But all of that seemed to escape him now. The only words he was able to force out were, "My brother." The two brothers embraced.

Stepping out of the chariot, Magnor stood at attention as Jael exited. As Jael's foot touched the ground, there was an explosion that shook the universe. It was followed by moments of quiet and uneasiness as those in the Kingdom were unsure of its origin.

Patho felt it, and fearful that Magnor or Jael were returning, he screeched out, "What the Pit was that?" No one answered, for all in the Pit had immediately taken cover. Jael's exit was very fresh in all their minds.

In the Kingdom, gasps began to be heard as attentions were drawn toward Turayn. What had started as a glow that was visible just after the explosion were now flames blazing through the atmosphere.

The Princes stood behind the King and Queen, all eyes were now on the flames. "What is that?" Quaine asked in a whisper. He hadn't intended to say it out loud; he had planned to avoid any attention this day.

"The Tree of Everlasting Life," replied Ferrul, who was standing closest to him. "The tree that ignited The Plan. It no longer has a purpose. Jael has made sure of that."

"The Tree of Everlasting Life?" Quaine asked, his eyes still fixed on the glow. "I thought that was just a story."

Ferrul smiled gently, "No, it is - or was - real." He looked over to his brother. This must be a blur to him, he thought. Ferrul felt a great sense of loss. Quaine has missed so much.

All that had been discussed, planned, and attempted. The conversations, the debates, the successes; he had not been there to participate in any of it.

Ferrul took a step closer to Quaine and speaking in a very soft and gentle voice began to explain, "The Tree of Everlasting Life was essential to ensure that Free Will was a part of Turayn from the beginning. Father will always give choices." Quaine stood expressionless, his gaze fixed on the flame. "After Konnory left the Garden, Father placed guards around it. There was recently a report of someone, or something, finding a way in and partaking of it. There is no confirmation as to who it was, but Father said it was time to destroy it."

"So Jael is its replacement?" Quaine asked stone-faced, looking towards Turayn.

"To a degree. Eating from that tree allows one to live forever; however, that forever is limited to Turayn." Quaine's head jerked toward Ferrul. "I know. Who would want to remain in Turayn forever?" he asked.

Konnory moved forward and stood at Jael's side. Putting his arm around his brother's shoulders as they watched the flames begin to decrease, he said, "Well done, my brother, well done. Welcome home!"

The others rushed forward. Jael suddenly found himself engulfed by four of his brothers. They had all lived for this moment. This was their victory, all of theirs. Jael greeted each one, but where was Quaine? Jael searched to find him.

Quaine remained well behind the King and Queen. Once in Jael's view, he separated himself from the others and made his way to Quaine's side. Quaine held his hand out in greeting. Jael took his hand, and then pulled Quaine into him. "Welcome home," Jael whispered.

The King and Queen cherished the moment. Waldemar and Tayten stood next to them on either side. Tayten was unsuccessfully doing his best to hold back tears. Waldemar was beaming with joy.

The King stepped forward, and their eyes locked. Turning and releasing himself from Quaine, Jael and the King embraced. With shouts of joy, the King and Jael were once again united. A wave of cheers spread across the crowd as the two embraced. Jael felt himself melting into the King's arms. Being wrapped in his arms was anchoring him once again. Every part of his being was being restored. He breathed deep renewing breaths as every part of him was being filled with the King. Jael felt Father begin to release him. He wanted to linger, he would be content being wrapped in Father's arms for eternity.

The King released Jael from his embrace. He took a step back, placing his hands on Jael's shoulders, the two stood, eyes locked again. There was no misty film covering his eyes, no tears needing to escape. Their silence spoke volumes. As the King stepped back, Jael saw the Queen. She was radiant. Jael stood, taking in her beauty; he felt his soul was being restored. As she opened her arms, Jael rushed toward her.

"My son," she said.

"Mother," Jael replied as he buried his head in her shoulder. Jael felt the King's hand on his back. Their strength permeated his entire being; if there had been any injury, any affect remaining upon him from his life in Turayn or his time in the Pit, it was being healed. Jael's re-entrance into the Kingdom would not be like that of the Fallen Souls, he had not requested forgiveness. He had gone to offer it.

Jael felt his mother begin to loosen her hold and he resisted. Putting her hands on his shoulders, she gently pushed against his resistance. Standing tall and strong in front of her, the Queen cradled his face in her hands. "You were the one," she said softly. "No one else was worthy of such a task."

A smile began to emerge on the King's face. As it grew, he could no longer contain his joy! Putting his head back, the King bellowed, "WELCOME HOME!"

Instantly the Princes broke out in celebration with shouts and cheers of victory. Those gathered around joined in with applause, cheering, and dancing. The celebration began to ripple out and spread through the entire Kingdom. Banners waving in the air and trumpets blasting announced his final homecoming.

The King took Jael by the arm and headed for the castle. As they passed Quaine, Jael grabbed his arm, forcing him to walk along. "I have so many questions for you," he said.

"For me? What do you want to know about me?" Quaine asked cautiously.

"We didn't get much chance to talk, and I want to know, when did you realize who you were?" Jael smiled as he continued to pull Quaine along. "And how did you get back so quickly?"

"Magnor had his hand in that one," Carasi responded from behind them.

Jael looked back to find Magnor, "So you finally worked?" he asked with a laugh.

"I helped," Konnory added proudly as he threw his hands in the air. The laughter echoed through the corridors. Even Quaine relaxed a little and broke into a small smile.

As they passed through the entrance to the castle, the King stopped. He motioned for the figure standing just inside the doors to step forward. As the man approached, Jael felt the connection. The King began to speak, but Jael stopped Him. "You don't have to tell me Father, I know who he is!" With those words, Jael greeted the man. "Thank you," he said as he bowed his head in acknowledgment.

"Thank me? Oh, no Sire, you are the one to receive all our gratitude," the man said, overcome with emotion.

What felt as if it were an eternity ago and yet only yesterday, this is the man who had given himself over to the King and welcomed Jael into Turayn.

"You are to join us, correct?" asked Jael, looking at Father for his consent.

"Of course, he is to join us!" assured the King. The King took the hand of the man, "You have my eternal gratitude for the protection and care you provided Jael when he entered Turayn."

"Sire, it was an honor," he replied.

The King took Jael's arm once again and continued down the hall leading to the Dining Room. Jael reached out for Quaine's arm to ensure he would not make an exit. The castle looked different. There was a brilliance about it. Each color jumped out at him.

The doors to the Dining Room were open and Jael could see the glow of the fire. How he had missed sitting around the table, conversing with his brothers, and eating together. As they approached the entrance, Jael expected they would turn in; but the King never slowed as he passed, causing Jael to jerk Quaine's arm to keep up. The only other room down this corridor was the Throne Room and it had been a very long time since it had seen any life.

The King stopped in front of its large, ornate doors. As the doors opened, the bustle of the room silenced. In unison, all in attendance turned toward the door. Jael waited for Father to go first, but to his surprise, Father never released Jael's arm. Taking a step in, Jael was forced to keep up. Quaine pulled away and Jael released him.

Their steps were slow and exact as the King escorted Jael into the room. A few paces in, Jael saw Waldemar and Tayten. Both men bowed down on one knee. Jael looked at Father for approval and with a nod, Jael rushed over to them. He reached down to grab both of their hands and brought them to their feet.

"Welcome home, Sir," said Waldemar.

"Well done! Well done, my son," said Tayten. Jael embraced both men. It was a day of rejoicing, a day of great celebration.

Taking his arm once again, the King continued their entrance. A few paces further, Jael realized that the King's purple carpet had been unrolled. The King and Queen were the only ones to have walked on its deep purple fibers. The King never hesitated; as He walked, Jael walked. From behind them, the room was filling up quickly with observers, their images blurred to Jael. Before them, the royal curtains which enclosed the King and Queen's thrones.

As they approached the end of the walkway, they stood looking forward. The royal curtains began to part. Those in attendance reacted to the addition; just to the right of the King's throne was a newly carved throne. Its beauty and detail were exquisite. Its carvings were bold, yet intricate. With one flowing gesture, the King directed Jael to his new position "No, Father," Jael protested as he looked back at the Queen. She bowed her head. Jael shook his and said, "This was meant for Palti."

"No. Palti will never sit here. This place was and has always been intended for you," assured the King. "Welcome home, Son."

Jael's new position was seated next to Father; a position that had never before existed. Before taking his seat, Jael could not help but inspect the workmanship of this elaborate throne. The detail of the carvings, it was like none other – Jael stopped. He looked around the room in search of someone. He must be there? Father said he was invited. They had just greeted him as they entered the castle.

Suddenly, Jael spotted him; he was standing just inside the doors. Jael recalled watching him work on that small chair in his workshed. It was the first thing that had allowed him to remember details of the Kingdom. The man gave Jael a gentle nod. Jael smiled and mouthed, "Thank you." Placing his hand over his heart, he bowed his head in reverence.

As Jael took his place next to the King, he saw the Throne Room from a new vantage point. Jael took his time looking around the room. To his left stood Konnory and Quaine, next to them stood Ferrul and Carasi. To the right stood the Captains of the army with Magnor at the head. Jael recognized the faces of each Captain. These were the men that had committed to protect him and The Plan. His triumph was theirs as well; he could feel the pride his brother had in his warriors.

Jael continued looking around the room. He paused, replaying in his mind what his eyes had just seen. Standing next to Magnor was a small figure, adorned in robes of the finest silk. Leaping from the throne he shouted, "Odella!"

"Welcome home." Odella knelt down and bowed her head. Jael helped her to her feet and they embraced. In one quick movement, the three held each other tightly. Tears were flowing throughout the room. Even the Captains began blinking rapidly to try to hold them back. After regaining his composure and with one final kiss for each, Jael returned to his new position.

Today was the greatest homecoming the Kingdom had experienced. A grand celebration would follow. No one cared if Patho heard, in fact, it was just the opposite. They wanted him to hear. They wanted him to question. They wanted him to be afraid. The Plan had worked! It was executed flawlessly. The final step was up to the King. At any time, He could seal Patho in the Pit. Until then, the Fallen Souls would continue to find forgiveness. The Kingdom would welcome home those that did. No one would be excluded. Forgiveness was available to all.

The King closed the tablet and sat in reflection.

Balbas was pacing just outside the doors as a million thoughts rushed through his head. *This is it! Never again. Why did I say yes? But what could I say? You don't tell the King "No". Konnory, it's all your fault. Why couldn't you just leave it? Why couldn't we just start fresh with this new assignment? I can't breathe, and I'm sweating. Insane, that's what I am, insane…*

"He is ready for you."

Balbas stopped cold. He wiped his forehead and rubbed his sweaty hands down his side. He took a deep breath and walked through the doors that were being held open for him. He blinked a few times in an effort to make the black spots that were blurring his vision disappear.

"Balbas, thank you," the King said.

Balbas bowed his head. "I came as soon as I received your request."

"Balbas, I'm not thanking you for coming. I'm thanking you for your work." Balbas' eyes widened. "It is a beautiful record."

"But Sire, surely someone else has been keeping record."

"Of course. You're surrounded by rooms filled with files and records. But those are facts, this is a story. A story as seen through the eyes of those who were watching." At a loss for words, Balbas simply bowed his head once again. "With your permission, I would like to place this in the King's library."

Balbas took a deep, nervous breath. He squinted his eyes to try and prevent the gush that was soon to follow. He had never seen the King's Library. He had heard of it, heard of its great content and select books. This had been his way of recording history. This was his way of remembering. The thought of it someday sitting on a shelf as a part of the King's collection had never entered his mind.

"May we never forget," said the King.

"May we never forget," Balbas repeated. "For those who left, and those who remained...may we never forget."

4

As the sun rose, Konnory and Jael walked along the seashore. "I spent as much time here as I could," Jael recalled.

"I can see why," Konnory said. "It's the mirror image of the lake just beyond the gardens."

Jael stopped in his tracks and began to look around at his surroundings. Slapping Konnory on the shoulder, he said with great enthusiasm, "You're right! Why didn't I see that before?"

"Perhaps you had more important things on your mind?" Konnory asked with a bit of sarcasm. "Come on, keep walking. It must be just up there."

Through the morning mist, Konnory saw the makings of a small fire. As they drew closer, Jael could smell the smoke and it warmed him. The Watchers had taken care in providing them with everything needed for the morning breakfast, including starting the fire. Jael knelt down, picked up a stick, and started poking the embers. Konnory settled on a rock close by. Jael began fanning the embers, creating a small billow of smoke which targeted Konnory.

Konnory began fanning the smoke away with his hand, but with little success. "Excuse me, I am sitting here," Konnory said. Jael just chuckled. "You're doing that on purpose, aren't you?"

"One cannot control the wind," Jael replied.

"I'm not so sure about that," Konnory said, still fanning the smoke from in front of his face. "Stop already!"

Jael chuckled once again, "You could move."

"You could stop! Oh, never mind," Konnory stood and moved out of the path of the smoke. He sat on the ground and watched Jael tend to the flames. He was very comfortable in this setting. The sun was now reflecting off the water and a mist was rising, as the warmth of the day began to replace the cool damp of the night.

"Where are they?" Konnory asked.

"They will be here," Jael answered as he lifted a large leaf that covered a pile of fish.

"How many are coming?" Konnory asked.

"It will all depend on their catch," Jael replied. With the embers now glowing, Jael began to place the fish on the fire.

"You've done this before," Konnory said, quite impressed at his brother's culinary skills.

"Yes, many times," Jael replied. Jael put his head back and took a deep breath. The salt air combined with the smell of the fire and scent of freshly smoked fish filled his nostrils. "Nothing like it. This is what Turayn was created to smell like."

"Ha, I wonder what Father would say about that."

"I believe He would agree with me, my brother. I doubt you would find any argument from Him."

Konnory continued to watch Jael as he prepared the meal. "What hold does the Temple have on the Humans?" Konnory asked.

"Where did that come from?"

"It's very apparent that the Temple and now even the Empire have a control on these Humans. I don't understand it, just thought you may have some insight," Konnory said.

"I thought it would be quite evident," Jael answered. "It's fear."

"Fear?" Konnory asked. "Fear of what?"

Jael thought for a moment. "Fear of being able to achieve."

Jael paused, pondering his words as he continued to poke the embers. "Fear of not being able to succeed at obeying the Law."

"The Law? You mean the laws of the land?" asked Konnory.

"No," Jael answered. "I refer to the Laws Father gave the Humans many years ago."

"But Father gave those as a way to show them that they could not possibly "do" anything to gain his approval; are you saying that the Humans are still trying to follow the Law on their own?"

"Yes. Like sacrifice, they have made the Law about themselves. The Temple uses it as a way to condemn the Humans. Some use it as a mark of how good they are in comparison to how bad others are. The new Empire has succeeded in giving the Laws degrees of evil. They have actually grouped them together. According to them, there are some Laws that, once broken, will never allow one to seek forgiveness."

"You're exaggerating, right?" Konnory asked. "Degrees of evil? That's absurd. It would be like saying those who left the Kingdom, but only stayed just outside the gates, were not as wrong as those who were further out. THEY WERE ALL OUTSIDE OF THE GATES!" Konnory's hands were flailing in the air.

Jael couldn't help but laugh at his dramatics. "Then there are those who simply use it as an excuse for not seeking forgiveness, claiming it's too difficult. Patho has succeeded on so many levels to distort the truth. He could sit back for the rest of eternity and let the Humans do his work." Jael added more fish to the fire.

Konnory was now on his feet and began to pace the shore line. He looked out over the water; in the distance he saw a small cluster of fishing boats. "But when Father gave the Law, he also reintroduced the importance of sacrifice."

"You'll find no argument here. Father made it very clear that it's impossible to keep all the Laws. It was an attempt to refocus their attention on sacrifice. He basically said 'You can't do it, so just make a sacrifice and all will be well,'" Jael said as he shook his head.

"They missed the sacrifice part and have focused on trying to keep all the Laws?"

"Exactly!" responded Jael. "The new Empire has further complicated it by attaching different degrees of punishment to each broken Law. Some of these poor souls will never understand Father's forgiveness because they have been told their entire life they will be living out their punishment."

Jael began removing fish from the fire. "Father made it clear – you have to obey all of them; if you break one you break them all. Only a handful understand; most just keep working, thinking that somehow they should be able to keep them all." Jael began fanning the flames until the embers were once again glowing. "I did it, you know."

"You did what?" Konnory asked.

"I followed all the laws."

"You did?"

"Yes."

"But," Konnory paused. "I don't recall that being part of the discussion."

"The time I spent in the Garden just before entering Turayn was time spent studying the Laws." Jael looked out over the water, "They should be coming soon."

"You followed all the Laws?"

"Is that so hard to understand?"

"A bit. That is no easy task," Konnory said. "Why?"

Jael laughed quietly, loving Konnory's need for explanation. "Someone had to!"

"Seriously," Konnory said. "Why?"

"The Law had become another hindrance for those seeking forgiveness. No Human could possibly keep it, but before Father could nullify its purpose, it had to be fulfilled."

"So it no longer exists?"

"Oh it exists, Father doesn't create things that lose their existence. But it no longer holds any connection for forgiveness. Those that follow the Law live very disciplined lives and in doing so, have a depth of understanding that is unmatched. In fact, their understanding and respect for Father is unparalleled." Looking up, he saw two boats coming closer to shore. "There are our guests now," he said.

Konnory sat quietly. "Did I confuse you?" Jael asked.

"No," Konnory replied. "I didn't realize this was also part of your time here."

Jael rose to meet a small group of fishermen who were walking toward them. "Come join us," he offered. Those were the same words he had said on the morning that he invited Ram and Micha to follow him.

The fishermen did not hesitate to accept the invitation. Sharing a morning meal on the shore was just as much a part of life to them as waking early each morning to head out for their catch. Jael and Konnory exchanged small talk with the men. It didn't take long before the conversation turned to the events of the recent past, and moments later the fishermen realized it was in fact Jael they were conversing with. With great excitement, the fishermen and Jael were reunited.

After meeting with each of his close followers, Jael instructed them to gather on a hill top. A place they had frequented as a group many times. Unbeknownst to them it would be the last time they would be together.

Late in the afternoon all were in attendance. The group stood clustered around Jael and Konnory. No one seemed to be concerned or questioned Konnory's presence. They all focused on Jael's every move. He greeted each one. Those in attendance were prepared with their list of questions, but once in Jael's presence, their memories faded. All they cared to do was listen to their teacher.

As Jael greeted Timothy, he held onto his hand and said, "Timothy, I told you that there would be a time coming shortly when you would stop questioning." Timothy nodded.

Jael leaned into him, "Timothy, open your eyes." Timothy looked at Jael with a confused expression. Jael once again gave the instruction but this time much slower and more defined. "Open-your-eyes!"

The others watched closely. Timothy began to look around, expressionless at first. His eyes grew wider. It was in exact proportion of the dropping of his mouth. Jael could feel his grasp tightening. At first, he only moved his eyes as if his body was frozen. Then he began to turn his head slowly from left to right.

Jael pried Timothy's hand open to release his arm. Timothy took a step backwards, and Jael reached out in preparation to catch him. Timothy tottered a bit, but eventually regained his balance. He then, ever so slowly, turned his entire body.

"What is it?" Gad asked. "What do you see?"

"There are thousands...no...there are millions," Timothy began. "Oh, they are magnificent. They are everywhere! I have never beheld such beauty, such strength, such power."

"What are?" Gad insisted.

"Them!" Timothy said, pointing his finger out into space. He turned completely around again. This time with both hands he gestured to encompass all around them. "All of them..."

Gad looked at Jael. Jael and Konnory looked at each other and smiled. "Gad, Timothy is looking at the Watchers," Jael assured.

"The Watchers?" Gad replied.

"Oh - they are magnificent!" Timothy said, lost in wonderment.

"They have been here from the beginning. They are your protection. They watch your every move. They surround you in order to prevent any outward attacks from Patho." Konnory said.

"Prevent attacks from Patho?" Thomas asked.

Timothy, still lost in amazement, did not hear any of the conversation. Jael reached over and laid his hand on Timothy's shoulder, who was eventually able to focus again. "Look further," Jael said, nodding his head in reassurance. Timothy once again looked questioningly at Jael. "Look - farther,"

Konnory made his way behind Timothy in preparation to catch him this time.

Timothy turned his head away. His knees buckled beneath him. Konnory reached out to steady him. Timothy was speechless. The others stood motionless. Timothy closed his eyes once and opened them. He did it again. The color left his face. Eventually, he whispered, "Warriors."

Konnory and Jael broke out in laughter. "It's like when we were kids and we coaxed Carasi into following our instructions in order to find the hidden treasure," Jael said softly to Konnory.

"Except this time - there really is something!" Konnory said.

Gad, who was becoming increasingly irritated, blurted out, "Warriors? Where? I don't see them."

Pointing to the horizon, Timothy said ever so quietly, as if a child whispering to his friend that there was something under his bed, "They are there. They stand at attention, shoulder to shoulder." Timothy turned around to see the entire circumference of the new sphere. In a very controlled and authoritative voice, he said, "They are the warriors of the Kingdom."

His words caused reaction from all. Each one's memory of the Kingdom began to open.

"These, too, have been here from the beginning of time. They not only protect, they are ready to attack Patho and any Pathonians at Jael's command. These are the warriors who will take Patho captive and seal him in the Pit," Konnory explained. "These are the warriors who were prepared to rescue Jael upon his command while he walked with you in Turayn."

With every word, Jael's followers became more and more aware of the power and authority this one who had walked with them, ate with them, led and taught them, possessed. Gad fell to his knees. Jael once again reached out and put his hand on Timothy's shoulder, bringing his attention back. Timothy was aglow. As he looked at Jael, he softly asked, "How will we survive without you?"

Jael smiled gently. "Timothy, you have seen what protects you from without. You never need fear that this protection will go away. The Watchers protect you, the Warriors protect Turayn."

"This doesn't stop Patho from attacking," Konnory said.

"No, it does not," said Jael. "He will never cease attacking. He will do all within his power to get you to doubt. His greatest attacks will be on your minds. He has one and only one goal, to get you to fear and doubt the King. Everything he does is for this purpose. Fear is his strongest means of attack. If he can succeed in doing this, even the slightest bit, he knows that your mind will finish the job."

"How do we fight him? How can we be powerful enough to withstand him?" Ram asked.

"You can't," Jael assured with a smile. "You can't on your own."

"Does that mean you will stay with us?" Micha asked.

"No," Jael said. "Not as you envision. The way back to the Kingdom, the ability to fight against Patho, the delight of walking with the King now comes from within." Jael paused. "The sacrifice has been made."

"When Jael gave himself as The Sacrifice, he brought an end to the requirement the King gave for sacrifice. He also broke the physical confines that stood between you and the King. He made it possible for the King to no longer walk with you, but to live through you. Your faith allows you to be guided; your desire to do good allows you to make a difference in other's lives. Your love for Jael and for the King allows you to forgive and love others in ways they have never known. Your desire to return to the Kingdom forces you to tell others of Jael's sacrifice."

Konnory had everyone's attention, including Jael's.

"Your soul is where the King abides. You must learn to listen to it. You must allow it to guide you, for it is the soul that hears the King's heart."

"It is from your soul that we will forever be connected," Jael said. "Protect it. Guard your heart and control your mind. You now have the ability to do so much good. Don't let it get lost. Don't let it get confused."

The group stood quietly. "We can't do this without you!" Benjamin proclaimed.

"But I'm not leaving. You no longer need me to walk with you; we are now connected from within," Jael said ever so reassuringly.

"Timothy, never forget what you witnessed today. You're not alone, you will never be alone. You must stop looking for the answer. You have everything you need."

Konnory stepped over to Jael and put his arm around his brother's shoulders. "It's time to go home."

"I know," said Jael, "It's not easy to leave them."

Jael embraced each, and each was reluctant to let him go. As Jael said his final goodbye, he stepped back from the group. Looking kindly at them he bid them good-bye, "I will see you in the Kingdom!"

The two brothers turned and began to walk away. Jael's followers stood motionless. They walked as if they were walking on a long incline, their feet no longer touching Turayn. Soon they began to blend into the horizon. The moment they disappeared from sight, there was a huge rush of wind.

The noise was deafening. They were unable to withstand its power, forcing each to the ground. It seemed to be an instant and yet an eternity. As each began to regain their composure, they were overcome with a power they had never felt. It brought strength that none had ever experienced. It also brought a peace that was unexplainable.

5

He's a Prince and a Fallen Soul," Ferrul said. "That's a combination we've not dealt with." Ferrul, Carasi, and Jael walked down the hall together. Their concern for Quaine's inability to adjust to his homecoming was wobbling on the edge of worrisome.

"But Father's made provision for him," Carasi replied. "He's been assigned to Tayten. He's in the castle where we can keep a close eye on him. But he's just not responding."

"Has anyone asked Tayten? I wonder what he would say." asked Jael.

"Tayten has been very closemouthed about the whole ordeal. I'm not sure if that is a good thing or bad," Ferrul replied. "He's still not comfortable being in the position he is in. Perhaps looking over the operations of the castle was too much for him."

"Never," said Carasi. "He's as qualified as anyone for that role. Give him time, I am sure he will find his way quickly. After all, he's been part of the place since we were kids. He's not the issue, it's Quaine – there's just something missing. He should be much farther along than he is."

"The natural process of death for the Human was intended to be an aging process," said Ferrul. "It is possible that the quick death he experienced could have prevented him from being prepared for his return."

"Don't get me wrong, I would love to blame this on Magnor if for no other reason than to watch his reaction, but others have died abruptly, not being given a chance to age," said Jael. "Their return was proof time was not hindered by the way they left Turayn. Could his last hours have been the cause? His last day was far less than normal."

"I hadn't considered that," Ferrul replied. "Remembering who he was may have had some lasting effect."

Jael stopped, forcing Ferrul and Carasi to do the same. "Not only that, I asked him to do something, that for a human, would have been emotionally overwhelming. Remembering the Kingdom combined with the torment he felt by the task. He faced so much those last few hours."

"It's possible," Carasi said, "but I don't think that is what we are seeing. He is holding on so tightly to his guilt. At times, he seems to still be Human." A few more steps and they were entering the Dining Room. Involuntarily, the three scanned the room,

"Looks as if he's missing another dinner," Carasi said.

That evening, dinner was served over cordial conversation. As dinner finished, the King asked Waldemar to call Tayten to join them. A short time later, Tayten entered. "Sire, what can I do for you?" he asked.

"Quaine has missed several meals with us recently. I wanted to make sure you were aware, and also, is this of any concern?" the King asked.

Tayten hesitated in his response. By his expression, those around the table knew he was becoming uncomfortable. "Sire, I wish I could say that Quaine is strengthening daily, but that doesn't seem to be the case. He is struggling." Tayten said.

"Thank you, Tayten. I know you are doing everything possible," the King replied. Tayten took his leave.

"He's struggling far too much," said Konnory.

"Would it help if I spoke with him?" Jael asked. No one responded.

Finally Waldemar spoke up, "Excuse me Sir, if I may, I don't believe that would help. I know very well what Quaine struggles with. Being confronted by you would most likely make it more difficult. When Tayten and I returned, you had not yet gone to Turayn. The guilt we brought back with us was great. I can only imagine Quaine's guilt is greater due to the simple fact that he saw what you were put through."

"And for that matter, assisted in putting me there," Jael said ever so solemnly.

"I'll speak to him," Konnory offered. "Thank you, son," the King replied.

The Pit had been in a state of upheaval since the day Jael walked out. Patho had forced Abaddon to remain with him until a plan of attack had been completed. Patho attempted to confine Serpent as well, but Serpent would have nothing of it. He showed up at his own choosing, for he would not be forced to do anything.

Patho ordered Abaddon and Secretary to find out how a request for redemption was made. He didn't really care about the details of how it was done, he had an alternative reason. Patho sent warlords out into the Darkness in order to find any Fallen Soul who was willing to talk. They were very forceful in their attempts. However, the only ones willing to offer any information were those who had found themselves hopelessly back in the darkness.

There was a great division even amongst these. One group was so overwhelmed with the anguish and torment that they became unresponsive. Patho's warlords were unable to get their attention, never mind get them to speak. Another group showed a bit more signs of life, but it was as if they were lost in great confusion. They refused to believe that they were once again in the Darkness.

It was the third group the warlords were able to obtain most of their information. This group was consumed with anger. Their anger was targeted toward the King. According to them, it was the King's responsibility to assure their return to the Kingdom. Three of these Fallen Souls agreed to provide information desired and had accepted an invitation to the Pit for further discussion.

Jael's departure left the Pit in shambles. The interior had been shaken to the core. Patho did not bother to make any repairs. His desk sat low enough to the ground to allow him to crouch and work, there was little other furniture. Dust and dirt covered the floor. Anytime anyone walked, a billow of filth was created.

Secretary and Abaddon had been crouched at the table for some time. Patho slithered between the conference area and his desk. He was insistent that the Fallen Souls would be questioned, yet he despised the thought that they would be in his Pit. "I don't want anyone calling them Fallen Souls!" he instructed.

"Who?" asked Secretary.

"The ones that are coming," Patho snarled.

"How should we address them?" Secretary asked in his consistently annoyed tone.

"Not by their Kingdom names!" Patho replied. "Call them something from Turayn."

"Like what?" Secretary asked. "Loir, Haddad, perhaps Timar." Patho glared at him. He wrinkled his noise and turned up his upper lip. "No, you don't like those?" Secretary asked with great boldness.

Abaddon cringed. He hated Secretary's boldness. The recent time that he had been forced to stay in the Pit had been agony. Patho and his new assistant, Secretary, were in a constant battle of words. Patho's previous assistant vanished one day; no one was ever able to locate him. It was thought that perhaps he had put in a request for forgiveness; if that were the case, it was believed that he would be a Pit asset once he entered Turayn.

Abaddon could no longer find any humor in Secretary's sarcasm; he only felt the pressure of keeping some order of control to prevent Patho from entering another tyrant.

Three dark and almost formless creatures made their way into the conference room at the appointed time. Each looking around in disgust, it was just as they had expected. "Sit down," instructed Secretary in a scolding manner. The three looked around. "Sit, didn't you hear me?" The three squatted to the ground in unison. The movement created a cloud of grime that took a while to settle.

"You are here today, to provide us information of the process for a Fallen Soul to request forgiveness," Abaddon said. "You will be addressed as, Sam, Syrus and Sul." He pointed to each as he informed them of their new names. The three gave him a blank stare. Secretary snorted.

Abaddon continued, "How are requests made?"

"IDIOTSSS!" Patho shouted with a hiss, never bothering to look up from his desk.

Abaddon stopped in anticipation of him continuing, he did not. Pointing to one of the Fallen Souls who had been newly named Sul, he said, "Tell us the process."

"A request is given to a Transporter or Messenger," Sul began. The other two remained expressionless. They knew very well that Sul did not have any idea what he was talking about; no one knew how such requests were made, they just were. They both felt that showing any sign of ignorance would be highly unadvisable.

"How is it given? What is it?" asked Secretary in very short and quick demands.

This time there was no answer. There was also no change in their expression. They could feel the urgency in Secretary's tone, but they were at a loss for words. Syrus slouched and smirked. Sam began to twitch ever so slightly. "Well?" insisted Abaddon.

Secretary took their silence as an answer. "What do you mean, you don't know? You did it, didn't you?" Secretary shouted,

"Another day in paradise," he snarled. Abaddon felt himself begin to tremble. Being stuck in the Pit with Patho was bad, interacting with Patho and Secretary was horrific. Adding Serpent to the group was worse than being sent back to the Kingdom. Turning his attention back to the three and desiring to move the moment forward, "Explain yourselves," he insisted.

"We don't know!" Sul shouted. Serpent hissed.

Syrus jumped in determined to take control of the situation. "The Messengers...they...they are responsible to make sure the Fallen Souls are given a request." The other two nodded, at least it sounded good, well, it sounded better than anything either of them could come up with. As far as they were concerned, sounding good was far better than being right. "Once the request was complete, a Transporter would take it back to the Kingdom." Syrus looked confident in his answer.

Abaddon closed his eyes and shook his head. He still didn't understand the process, but unless Patho or Secretary requested clarification, he certainly wasn't going to. "How long do you wait?" he asked.

"There is no set time," Sam replied. "You just wait."

"For what?" Secretary asked.

Sam thought it he would be if he better join the conversation, "For your time." He hesitated finding little else to say. Serpent found his response quite humorous.

Secretary slowed his speech and said very deliberately, "What – happens – when – it – is – your - time?"

Sul's eyes widened as if the lights had just turned on."It's very abrupt," he said. "In a flash, you're pulled from the darkness, you spend a great deal of time in a holding place, and then you find yourself in Turayn. You begin as a small one." The idea of small ones made Sul squirm as if the Pit were suddenly overcome with them.

"Small what?" Secretary snapped. Abaddon waited for the anticipated remark from Serpent. He was surprisingly disappointed.

"A small human," Syrus said.

"Uh," Sam twitched at the thought.

"There is never any recollection of the darkness or of any time prior to entering Turayn. All you know is your life there."

"Where does forgiveness come in?" Abaddon asked.

As if programmed, Sul repeated, "A Human must seek forgiveness from the King."

"Through sacrifice, correct?" Abaddon asked.

"Yes, through sacrifice," Sul said with a nod.

"Enough!" Patho shrieked. "You've told me nothing of any importance. It all sounds so Kingdomly." Patho spit. "I despise the King's order. I don't care how they get a request or how they get forgiveness." Patho stood up and began to pace, dust and grime billowing out beneath his feet. "We have to stop them from ever leaving the darkness."

"What are you suggesting?" Abaddon asked.

"Find them! Find any Fallen Soul that has requested forgiveness!" Patho raged.

"And do what with them...kill them?" Serpent taunted.

"Confine them!" Patho commanded. "We'll construct a holding chamber..."

"Similar to this one?" Secretary said under his breath. Abaddon cringed again.

"How do we determine who's made a request?" Abaddon asked.

Patho looked at the Sul, Syrus and Sam. "We need spies. I'm sure these idiot...these three who sit in front of you would be honored to serve as spies." Patho said looking at the three.

Patho's look sent a chill through the room. Sam was now twitching uncontrollably. Spy for Patho – it sounded devilishly exciting. Secretary slammed the table with his hand and Abaddon belched. The three newly appointed spies jerked. This inquisition had just become a project. It was a project that neither Abaddon nor Secretary wanted to partake in, but both knew very well they would have no choice.

"You can go now!" Secretary ordered. Sul, Syrus and Sam remained crouched in a state of confusion. *Go where?* they all thought. Their moment's hesitation was not acceptable to Secretary. "What are you waiting for? Get out!" he shouted.

The three quickly stood and turned toward the door. Sam, however, was so befuddled he found himself turned away from the door, he was facing Serpent. Serpent sneered. Sam did an about face and finding a gap between he and his partners, attempted to bolt through it.

"WAIT!" shouted Secretary. Sam stopped cold. The other two had made it out. He didn't turn around. He just stood there like a salt statue with his back to the room. "One of you must report every day to my desk for further instructions!" Sam remained motionless. "GO!" shouted Secretary. And in a flash, Sam was gone.

"Oh, that will surely be the delight of each day to see those blundering idiots," Secretary said as he gathered his papers. Assuming that the meeting was over, Abaddon took his leave quickly. Secretary stood and turned toward Patho who was slumped behind his desk, he waited a moment for further instruction but when there wasn't any, he too left the room.

which was almost a screeching yell. Just then, Serpent entered the room.

"You're late!" Patho bawled.

"NO!" Serpent glared back at Patho. "I'm here," he said very slowly and pronounced.

Secretary leaned toward Abaddon, "Another day in paradise," he snarled.

Abaddon felt himself begin to tremble. Being stuck in the Pit with Patho was bad. Interacting with Patho and Secretary was horrific. Adding Serpent to the group was worse than being sent back to the Kingdom. Turning his attention back to the three and desiring to move the moment forward, "Explain yourselves," he insisted.

"We don't know!" Sul shouted. Serpent hissed

Syrus jumped in determined to take control of the situation. "The Messengers...they...they are responsible to make sure the Fallen Souls are given a request." The other two nodded, at least it sounded good, well, it sounded better than anything either of them could come up with. As far as they were concerned, sounding good was far better than being right. "Once the request was complete, a Transporter would take it back to the Kingdom." Syrus looked confident in his answer.

Abaddon closed his eyes and shook his head. He still didn't understand the process, but unless Patho or Secretary requested clarification, he certainly wasn't going to. "How long do you wait?" he asked.

"There is no set time," Sam replied. "You just wait."
 "For what?" Secretary asked.

Sam thought it would be better if he joined the conversation, "For your time." He hesitated, finding little else to say. Serpent found his response quite humorous.

Secretary slowed his speech and said very deliberately, "What – happens – when – it – is – your - time?"

Sul's eyes widened as if the lights had just turned on. "It's very abrupt," he replied. "In a flash, you're pulled from the darkness, you spend a great deal of time in a holding place, and then you find yourself in Turayn. You begin as a small one." The idea of small ones made Sul squirm, as if the Pit were suddenly overcome with them.

"Small what?" Secretary snapped. Abaddon waited for the anticipated remark from Serpent. He was surprisingly disappointed.

"A small human," Syrus said. "Uh," Sam twitched at the thought.

"There is never any recollection of the darkness or of any time prior to entering Turayn. All you know is your life there."

"Where does forgiveness come in?" Abaddon asked.

As if programmed, Sul repeated, "A Human must seek forgiveness from the King."

"Through sacrifice, correct?" Abaddon asked. "Yes, through sacrifice," Sul replied with a nod.

"Enough!" Patho shrieked. "You've told me nothing of any importance. It all sounds so Kingdomly." Patho spit. "I despise the King's order. I don't care how they get a request or how they get forgiveness." He stood up and began to pace, dust and grime billowing out beneath his feet. "We have to stop them from ever leaving the darkness."

"What are you suggesting?" Abaddon asked.

"Find them! Find any Fallen Soul that has requested forgiveness!" Patho raged.

"And do what with them...kill them?" Serpent taunted.

"Confine them!" Patho commanded. "We'll construct a holding chamber..."

"Similar to this one?" Secretary asked under his breath. Abaddon cringed again.

"How do we determine who's made a request?" Abaddon asked.

Patho looked at Sul, Syrus, and Sam. "We need spies. I'm sure these idiots...these three who sit in front of you, would be honored to serve as spies." Patho said.

Patho's look sent a chill through the room. Sam was now twitching uncontrollably. Spy for Patho – it sounded devilishly exciting. Secretary slammed the table with his hand and Abaddon belched. The three newly appointed spies jerked. This inquisition had just become a project. It was a project that neither Abaddon nor Secretary wanted to partake in, but both knew very well they would have no choice.

"You can go now!" Secretary ordered. Sul, Syrus and Sam remained crouched in a state of confusion. Go where? they all thought. Their moment's hesitation was not acceptable to Secretary. "What are you waiting for? Get out!" he shouted.

The three quickly stood and turned toward the door. Sam, however, was so befuddled he found himself turned away from the door, facing Serpent. Serpent sneered. Sam did an about-face, and finding a gap between he and his partners, attempted to bolt through door.

"WAIT!" shouted Secretary. Sam stopped cold. The other two had made it out. He didn't turn around. He just stood there like a salt statue with his back to the room. "One of you must report to my desk every day for further instructions!" Sam remained motionless. "GO!" shouted Secretary. And in a flash, Sam was gone.

"Oh, that will surely be the delight of each day to see those blundering idiots," Secretary said as he gathered his papers. Assuming that the meeting was over, Abaddon took his leave quickly. Secretary stood and turned toward Patho, who was slumped behind his desk. Secretary waited a moment for further instruction but when there wasn't any, he too left the room.

Serpent settled into the corner, crouching down in a most uncomfortable position.

After Sul, Syrus, and Sam had reluctantly but dutifully reported daily for several days, Patho called Secretary into his office. As he entered, Patho said, "Is anyone waiting out there?"

Secretary turned back to look, "No, there isn't anyone here," he said. Patho motioned for Secretary to come closer.

"I have a mission for you. You can't tell a soul, especially a fallen one! Find a request, I don't care how you do it, but find a request. It must be made in Abaddon's name," Pathos said.

Secretary took a step back. "Abaddon?" Secretary asked.

"SHHH, QUIET!" Patho sneered. "Yes, Abaddon. Get it made!"

Secretary stood for a moment, shaking his head. "All right Sire, but I'm not sure you can make a request for someone else. And...Abaddon isn't a Fallen Soul."

6

The Throne Room had taken on a new life. It was once again alive with conversation, discussion, and decision-making. Waldemar entered the room. In his hand was a note. He offered it to the King with a look of great concern.

The King reached out, and taking it from Waldemar asked, "Is this of interest?" Waldemar shrugged his shoulders. The King opened it carefully. He read it slowly and then read it again. "Do you know where Magnor is?" he asked.

"I passed him in the hall a short time ago. He was heading to the Dining Room."

"Call him. I believe he may need to be a part of this. Who delivered this to you?"

"Two Commanders, my Lord. They are waiting in the hall," Waldemar said.

"Ask them to wait a few moments longer. I don't want to get started without Magnor."

Waldemar walked over to an attendant standing by the door. "I'll find Magnor," he said. "Please relay to the commanders that the King will see them shortly.

Both men left the room. Waldemar headed down the hall and entered the Dining Room as Magnor sat down at the table; before him was a newly poured beverage and a small plate of food.

"Sorry, Sir, but the King is asking for you. Seems there has been a request for an audience, and he feels you should be in attendance," Waldemar said with a slight bow.

Magnor looked down at his plate and then up to Waldemar. "All right," he said, as he pushed his chair back and rose from his seat. He lifted his goblet and took a refreshing taste, then grabbed a roll and followed Waldemar. "This will have to do for now," he said, as he headed out of doors.

As they approached the Throne Room, Magnor recognized the two in waiting. These were the two commanders who oversaw the requests from the Fallen Souls. Upon seeing Magnor, both stood at attention. Magnor nodded, "Commanders," he said as he passed. Waldemar reached for the door, and Magnor now shared his concerned look as he entered.

"Hello, Father," Magnor said as he approached the King.

"Didn't take you from anything important, I trust?" the King asked.

"No. Nothing that I can't go back to," Magnor replied, tossing the roll in the air as if it were a ball. "Do we know what they want?" Magnor caught the ball of bread. He examined it and then tossed it to Waldemar, "I don't know why I thought I would have a chance to eat it." Waldemar caught it, but unsure what to do with it, looked around for a place to set it. He tossed it to an attendant waiting at the door. The attendant caught it with great pride, but suddenly found himself unsure as to what was expected of him.

"Have we finished our little game of toss?" the King asked. Magnor chuckled. The King caught Magnor's glance, "It could be what we were expecting." Magnor's demeanor instantly changed.

There was a long pause as the room become still and revenent. The King motioned for Waldemar to show the two visitors in. As they approached, the King greeted them, "I believe the last time you requested an audience, it had to do with the Others, and perhaps a multitude?"

The two shared looks of uneasiness as the memories of their last visit began to resurface. The Others? The multitude? As light began to illuminate their thoughts, their expressions broke into pleasant recollection. "Yes, Sire, it did." The two recalled the strange request.

"Do we know what happened with that, or should I say, those interesting requests?" the King asked.

"Only that we had mixed up the names. Multitude was the name of their leader, not the definition of the size of the group. However, we do believe it is a very large group of Others; may actually number in the thousands," replied the first.

"We don't believe we have seen any evidence that they have been in Turayn or returned to the Kingdom," said the other.

The King nodded in assurance with a hint of intrigue. "What brings you here today?" asked the King.

The men shifted slightly, the first waiting for the second to respond. "In the past, we have received a few petitions requesting the removal of the initial request," one of the commanders began.

Magnor held his hand up to stop the conversation. "Requesting to remove the original request for redemption? How often does this happen?" he asked.

"It has been very rare," the other commander replied.

"What would make a Fallen Soul do such a thing?" Magnor asked, looking at the King for insight.

"One can only imagine," replied the King. Turning his attention back to the commanders, "Remind me, what happens to such requests?"

"They are stamped with Upon Request – Request Denied." said the first commander. "They are then filed separately.

"And you say this is a rare occurrence?" asked the King. "Yes, it has been," was the reply. Magnor raised his brow.

"Sire, it was brought to our attention a short time ago that such requests had suddenly increased. We have now been watching very closely, and indeed such requests are increasing," said the first commander.

"Increasing at a rather startling rate," said the other.

The King and Magnor were still. "Do you know of any reason?" the King finally asked.

"We do not."

"This can't be good," Magnor said, addressing the King directly.

"No," said the King in agreement.

"What would be causing them to act in such a way? What is he doing?" asked Magnor.

The two commanders looked a bit uncomfortable. "There is no way for us to know what is happening out there," one of them replied.

"I know, I'm sorry, I wasn't directing that question to you," Magnor said reassuringly. "We knew he wouldn't take all this lying down. But I am surprised that he has moved so quickly. He's up to something!"

The room grew still and silent as those in attendance became drawn into the conversation. "Thank you for bringing this to our attention," the King said, breaking the silence. "Keep a close eye on it. I believe Carasi will want numbers."

"Yes," continued Magnor, "that will be important. Have someone begin a count; we'll need to know just how many we are talking about."

The King looked toward Magnor, "You may just get your battle after all," he said.

"This is not what I had in mind!" Magnor responded.

King looked down at the note and then turned his attention back to the commanders, "Thank you. We will need regular updates. If there are any changes, please communicate them to Waldemar." Waldemar's head jerked when he heard his name. He looked at the King questioningly. "Looks like you have a new assignment!" the King replied with a nod.

"Yes, Sire, we will stay on top of it." The two saluted both the King and Magnor before taking their leave.

The room was still once again. Each in attendance envisioning what could possibly be happening outside the gates. "Call Carasi and Ferrul," the King said. An attendant left immediately to do so. "Are Konnory and Jael back?"

"No. I expect them shortly," Waldemar replied.

"As soon as they return, send them in. They will want to be a part." The King looked down at the note still in his hands.

"Let the staff know we'll be in the Dining Room – this could take a while."

"Yes, Sire." Waldemar said. He looked toward the exit, searching for another attendant. One stood next to the door. With another nod, the attendant took his leave.

"Father, we'll need Odella and Quaine," Magnor said with a huge sigh.

"Does that bother you?" the King asked.

"Odella – no. Quaine, I'm not sure. Maybe this will be the thing to get him...back," replied Magnor, shaking his head.

"Odella and the Queen are in the gardens. Tayten should know where Quaine is," offered Waldemar.

"Very good," said the King. "Inform the Queen when you find them. I'm not sure if she will choose to be a part," the King said with a smile. Another attendant left the room.

"You don't have a secret notebook somewhere with this all planned out?" Magnor joked.

"No – not this one," the King answered. "But I do believe this one is yours." His look gave Magnor a slight quiver. "Hope you didn't have anything planned in the very near future."

"No, just a plate of food."

"Good! You'll be able to do both," the King said as he stood. "Shall we then?"

"After you," Magnor said, as he motioned the King to go ahead. As Magnor passed Waldemar, he reached out and grabbed his arm. "Don't think for a moment you are not involved in this one. If I'm in, you're in!"

The King laughed with delight.

7

Magnor held a tight grip on Waldemar as they made their way out the doors and down the hall.

A ripple of energy radiated through the castle. It was a sense that something unusual was happening, something unexpected, and possibly even something concerning. Waldemar pulled himself away from a reluctant Magnor as they entered the Dining Room.

"It's my duty to inform everyone of the meeting," Waldemar said.

"Make sure you are included in the collected!" Magnor instructed to Waldemar's back as he headed down the corridor. Waldemar waved his hand as he picked up his pace and rounded the corner.

King and Magnor entered the Dining Room and took their respected seats. Carasi was the first to respond to the summons and the next to enter the room.

"What's bringing us together this time?" he asked.

"Do you know where Ferrul is?" the King asked.

Carasi walked over to his chair and then paused, he thought for a moment, "No, as a matter of fact, I don't" he answered. His thinking state was interrupted by Konnory and Jael's laughter as they came down the hall.

"Welcome back," offered the King as the two entered the room. "Trust your mission was successful?"

"Most certainly," Konnory replied.

Magnor settled in, and as he reached for the carafe he began, "Father and I had some visitors this afternoon..."

"Let's wait until everyone is here." the King interrupted. He walked over to the window and looked out across the gardens. The Queen and Odella were walking arm in arm. He watched as Waldemar entered the garden. His quick pace made him look like he was gliding across the path. As he approached the two strollers, he bowed and then began to talk and point back to the castle. "Mother and Odella are coming in now."

The remainder of the group followed soon after and each took their place in the Dining Room.

Quaine entered with Tayten. Tayten motioned for him to take his seat at the table; Quaine did so with great hesitation. Tayten moved around the room in preparation for dinner. After assuring that everyone had arrived, Waldemar entered.

The King raised his eyebrows as he looked at Waldemar's chair. Waldemar hesitantly made his way over and took his place. "It's good to have you here," the King said.

"Now, what has brought us here?" Ferrul inquired.

"We had a visit today from the two commanders who oversee the requests of the Fallen Souls."

"Is there an issue?" Carasi asked. "Or are there just more Others who are sick of Patho?"

"As expected, Patho is on the move," answered Magnor.

The King looked around at each of the Princes. "As you recall," he began, "we made a provision for any Fallen Soul who has requested forgiveness to petition that such a request be removed."

"Wait," blurted out Odella, "They can revoke their requests?"

"What would make them do that?" asked Waldemar. "I can't imagine any of them doing such a thing."

"This has happened? Odella asked.

"According to the commanders it has not been a frequent request," Magnor replied as he reached out to take Odella's hand.

"Apparently, there is a problem..." Jael said.

"There is," answered the King. "There has been an unexpected increase in such requests." Waldemar and Odella gasped in unison.

"Clearly, he is on the move." Konnory said.

"We're assuming that Patho is doing something to force these Fallen Souls to remove their original request," Magnor said. "We do not know what that something is."

The King looked directly at Quaine, Odella and Waldemar, "Do you have any idea as to what he could be up to?"

Odella was the first to speak, "No. Patho left us alone. We never saw him. In the beginning, Abaddon and a few of the warlords would make their way through the Fallen Souls, but they never interacted with us."

"Do you recall any Fallen Soul mentioning such an action?" asked Carasi.

"There was one," Quaine answered. The group was surprised, and relieved, that he was joining in the conversation. "He had said he wanted to be part of the Pit, but wasn't sure if he would be accepted. His reasoning for making a request was to cover his bases as he put it."

"Do you know what happened?" Ferrul inquired.

"He was accepted into the Pit," Quaine answered. "As soon as he received Patho's approval, he went into a panic, trying to figure out how to remove his request. "'The last thing I want is forgiveness' were his last words." The absurdness of these words brought a heaviness to the entire room. "He's serving somewhere in the Pit."

Jael shook his head ever so slowly, "It must be Secretary. That one is evil!"

"Quaine, you were the most involved in these requests. What do you think Patho is doing?" the Queen asked.

"I'm not sure," he said quietly.

"You're not sure or you don't care?" Carasi blurted out. Ferrul strengthened his arm and placed it in front of Carasi's chest to stop him. Carasi eased back.

"Quaine, you have more insight than any of us concerning these requests. We only see the final result. What do you think Patho is doing?" Jael asked.

Quaine shifted in his chair. He took a deep breath, "He's torturing them. He's making threats that must be worse than the anguish of living in the darkness. It isn't beyond him to be holding them captive," Quaine said with great certainty.

"Torturing?" the Queen asked.

"Yes. He must have found a way," Quaine responded. "I can't imagine what that could be. Besides that one incident, I did not come in contact with anyone who wanted to stay...out there."

"What about those who returned to the darkness?" Konnory asked.

Whether he wanted to or not, Quaine was now the expert.

"Anyone who returned to the darkness after being in Turayn separated themselves from those who had not yet been," Quaine replied. "They could be involved. I had very limited interaction with any of them."

"But you did have some?" Mother asked.

"Yes, I did," Quaine said with a sorrowful tone. "You can't imagine how they changed entering the darkness the second time." Quaine closed his eyes. Waldemar could see that he was beginning to shake a bit. This happened on the few occasions when Quaine allowed himself to remember.

"Thank you," said Magnor with great sincerity. There was a collective sigh throughout the room. Anyone who wasn't already sitting back in their chairs did so. Several looked at Carasi, who simply replied with a shaking of his head.

"We need to know what he is up to," Magnor finally said.

"Easier said than done," said Ferrul. "It will require going out into the Darkness. Who's going to volunteer to do that?"

"The Messengers and Transporters do that already," Konnory said.

"But," Carasi began, "that is for a short period of time and if they are not going to Turayn, they stay very close to the Kingdom. Whatever Patho is doing, he's going to try to keep it a secret as long as possible. We can put the Messengers on alert, but it's doubtful that they will be able to give us an eye witness."

"I don't believe there is a Fallen Soul..." Odella paused, "I don't believe one of the Redeemed would be willing to go back out there."

"No," said the Queen, "and we would never expect them to."

"I know we could find a regiment that would be willing to, but that would appear as an attack," said Magnor. "I could ask for volunteers. It's likely that we would have many. Any warrior who still has family missing would do anything to get them back." This seemed to be the first possible solution.

"I have a question," the Queen said as she raised her index finger as if asking for recognition. "Do we know what possible effects from spending any length of time in the Darkness could have?"

Carasi looked at her. This was a brilliant question. The Fallen Souls came back changed. It had been assumed that this was due to their regrets of leaving the Kingdom. Could it be more?

The Other's had changed in appearance. It took time, but it was certainly an effect.

"No," Carasi answered with great certainty, "we don't!"

"We have warriors out there," Konnory said.

"Yes, but they are protected. They stand side by side, creating a secure chain. I've stepped into that chain, the energy and power that is created by their connection is protection enough," Magnor said. "Sending one or two out alone would not offer such protection."

"Do we need to know what Patho is up to in order to lay out a plan?" Waldemar asked.

The King slapped the table, bringing life and energy back into the room. "No, we don't!" he responded. "We can create a place for any Fallen Soul to retreat to until they enter Turayn."

"In the Kingdom?" Odella asked.

"No," said Quaine. "In the Darkness."

The King leaned forward. "Go on," he encouraged.

"We can create a protected area just outside the gates. It won't take long for the word to spread through the Fallen Souls that such a place exists," Quaine said.

"Are you suggesting that we build something?" Carasi asked.

"No," replied Waldemar. "Magnor just described its borders. We use warriors to protect the area, just as they do around Turayn. Within their protection, Fallen Souls can safely wait."

"Does this hinder or affect their entrance into Turayn?" Jael asked.

"I don't believe it would," added Carasi. "They enter Turayn with no memory. It doesn't matter where they are before they enter."

"Unless they are without a request," Quaine said softly.

"Yes, my brother, you are right," said Jael. "Once again we find ourselves needing to make a plan that will allow those who left the Kingdom to return. We have to do it, unless you...," Jael looked directly at the King, "...are willing to end it all now."

"Please no," requested Odella.

The King was moved by Odella's pleading, "No worries, my dear," he said. "This is not the time to end it. That is still in the future." Tayten stepped into the room and bowed slightly. "We are ready," confirmed the King. Tayten took his leave.

"Magnor, it looks as if you have the beginning of your battle plans. I'm sure you, Carasi and Ferrul will have a detailed outline by morning. Waldemar will make himself available." The King gave an insecure Waldemar a nod. "Odella, thank you for your willingness to participate. And Quaine, your insight is invaluable; I trust that you will assist in the planning.

As the King finished, the doors opened. A stream of attendants and servers entered the room. In an instant, the candles were lit, serving pieces were set out, and the room was filled with the delicious smells that accompanied the meal.

As Tayten passed behind his chair, Quaine rose slightly. Tayten put his hand on his shoulder, pushing him back down and said, "We can handle this one without you. Enjoy your dinner Sir." Quaine looked toward Waldemar. With a slight nod, Waldemar gave his approval.

The King took it all in. He reached to take the Queen's hand. His dinner table was growing in number and he was delighted.

8

It was mid-morning as Waldemar walked down the hall toward the Throne Room. As he approached the Dining Room doors, he could hear the exchange of conversation. *They've not left the Dining Room,* he thought to himself. *They should have moved to the Throne Room by now.*

As Waldemar drew closer to the door, the muddled noise became well-defined. He chuckled to himself. "I guess we will be meeting in here again today," he said. As he entered the room, the King glanced up in acknowledgment, but returned his attention back to Konnory and Jael; the three were deep in conversation.

"I believe I have what I need," Konnory said. "Jael are you sure you won't accompany me?" Jael looked up at Father.

"No," replied Father, "he will not. I'm certain that you and Balbas have it all well under control."

"I'm not sure if 'well under control' and Balbas can be used at the same time," Ferrul added.

"You'd be surprised," Konnory said.

"Don't think for a moment I don't want to go with you," Jael said. "I miss them all so dearly. But it is best not to. Besides, it gives you a purpose now," Jael said in jest.

"One should never be without a purpose," Konnory jested. "I'll be on my way." Sliding his chair back, Konnory stood and began walking toward the door.

"I'll be eager to hear your report," Jael said as he watched Konnory. Without turning around, Konnory raised his hand in acknowledgment, then pushed the door open and left the room.

"Alright then," the King said, "I believe it's time to begin our day's work."

Waldemar was standing close to the door, expecting those in attendance to begin moving toward the Throne Room. As he turned around, he realized that none of the Princes were making any attempt to leave. Instead of the King rising from his chair, he seemed to be settling in. Waldemar smiled as he realized that the Dining Room had once again become the planning room. He reached for the door.

"Are you leaving us?" asked the King.

Waldemar turned around. "I must check to see if anyone is in the Throne Room," he answered with a smile. The King nodded in approval.

Down the hallway, Waldemar was met by a steward exiting the Throne Room. "Where are they?" he asked.

"The King and Princes will be meeting in the Dining Room today," Waldemar replied. "Please inform the others that they shall be served around the table today."

"Today?" said the steward with a grin.

"Yes, today, and most likely tomorrow as well."

Waldemar could not help but think of the recent events in the Kingdom. He frequently caught himself thinking things were getting back to normal, but what was normal? So much had changed.

The Fallen Souls continued to find their way home. With each return, the Kingdom somehow changed. Jael had fulfilled his commitment. He was Jael, yet different. In the Throne Room, he now sat at the right hand of the King. A position which had not existed prior to his return from The Pit.

Konnory was beginning to make his trips to Turayn. He would be there to ensure Jael's message of forgiveness and grace was not hindered. There were those who were committed to distorting Jael's purpose. Konnory was determined to minimize their control in Turayn.

Magnor had received Odella back. They were the same, and yet, they were very different. Odella was in many ways stronger and wiser. At the same time, she seemed more fragile. Magnor was facing a battle, and it was not the one he had been anticipating.

Quaine was home. It was wonderful to have him back. There wasn't a Fallen Soul that was not aware of the role Quaine played in requesting forgiveness from the King. As each Fallen Soul returned to the Kingdom, they requested an audience with Quaine; each wanting to express their gratefulness for making their requests known. Each request was answered, but the audience denied. Quaine wanted no part of the appreciation.

Waldemar knew too well the struggle each Fallen Soul had in accepting forgiveness. It was a battle in and of itself. Waldemar worried at times that Quaine may never fully be free of the guilt he carried for leaving the King.

Palti was still missing. There had been no reports of his entrances into Turayn. This wasn't surprising, as no one was to know which Fallen Souls inhabited the human bodies. Waldemar assumed that Palti's entrance would somehow be noticed. He knew that the King longed to hear something, anything of Palti.

Waldemar entered the Dining Room just in time to hear Carasi say, "I think it's a brilliant idea!"

"Waldemar," said the King, "I believe we will be meeting in here today." Waldemar nodded. "In fact, let's just plan that we'll be in here until further notice."

"Yes, Sire," replied Waldemar, "I'll make sure everyone is informed." He smiled. As Waldemar stood facing the table and those that were seating around it, he had a great sense of confidence. Even with the changes he had observed and felt, the King was still and would always be the King. Waldemar would forever serve, love and honor him in any way he would be allowed to. Waldemar took his seat.

Jael's followers in Turayn had grown in number, but not without great resistance for the Empire and Temple Leaders. Jael's closest followers were growing bolder, and with that boldness came additional attacks against them.

Communities of believers were established within each city. They cared for one other, assisting whenever there was a need. They spread Jael's teachings. No matter how hard the Empire worked to stop them, the message of forgiveness and grace continued.

As Konnory entered Turayn, the Watchers directed him to a small meeting that was being held discussing the fusion of grace and the King's laws. When he arrived at the location, he quietly entered. Standing in the back, he observed the small group of men and women, about 20 or so, sitting in a circle in the middle of the room. They seemed unaware that the number of observers were growing, and the room was filling quickly.

Konnory slowly made his way to the center of the room with the intent to join in the discussion.

"The King's law is no longer important," someone said.

"No longer important? Are you mad?" asked another.

"Jael came to fulfill the King's law."

"I agree. When he died, so did the law."

"Nonsense!"

"Without the law, our world would be out of control."

"Do you assume that it is in control now?"

Konnory listened intently. "Do you believe the laws are no longer important?" he asked.

"No, they are very important," several responded.

"But they are not necessary?" Konnory asked.

"They are both important and necessary..."

"But Jael fulfilled them. We no longer have to follow them in order to receive forgiveness," said another.

Konnory continued listening as the group debated. Time past and the number of observers grew. Konnory felt as if he was hearing the same questions and answers repeatedly with no resolve.

"If the King's laws are important and necessary, yet they are not required for forgiveness, why do you continue to follow them?" Konnory asked. There was a moment of silence. Konnory felt as if he had perhaps broken into their endless thought cycle.

"I believe that is what this discussion is all about," one of them answered.

"Some of us don't follow them any longer," said another.

"I would beg to differ with you on that one," Konnory said. "You do follow them."

"Truly, some of us have put them aside."

Konnory reached over and grabbed the arm of the woman sitting next to him. "If I were to cut her throat right now, what would you do?"

"We would have you arrested!" The group was instantly in agreement.

"Why? If you no longer feel the King's law is necessary or important, why would you react in that way?" Konnory asked.

"Because it is wrong," someone responded.

"Not if there isn't a law!" Konnory said. Again the room was quiet, but not for long.

"That's nonsense. That's not what we are discussing anyway."

Konnory looked up at the Watchers who were surrounding the room and shook his head. He sat quietly once again. Time passed, and the debate continued. It seemed endless. Konnory's patience was wearing thin. He allowed a bit more time to pass before he stood to take his leave. Virtually unnoticed by those debating, Konnory made his way through the crowd and out the door. Once outside, he looked back toward the group, shook his head and began to walk away.

"You must be patient with them," a voice said from behind him.

Konnory stopped and turned around, expecting to see Jael. "I thought you weren't com..." It wasn't Jael.

"He grew impatient with them as well," the man said. "It may take some time; the human is a simple and complicated creation." The man held out his arm in greeting. "I don't believe we have met. I'm James."

"James? You are the leader of the believers here, correct?" Konnory asked.

"Yes. I am responsible for the group in this city," James answered.

"Quite a responsibility," Konnory remarked.

"Yes, yes it is," James replied.

"Do you know who I am?" Konnory asked.

"Not exactly. I believe you are not one of us, however," James answered. "You look like him. There are similarities in your eyes."

"Look like who?" Konnory asked.

"Jael," James replied.

"You knew him well?" asked Konnory.

"Yes, better than most. I am – or was his older brother."

"His older brother, then you did know him well," Konnory said, as he let his guard down and began to grin.

"Apparently, not as well as you - from your expression," James said. James began to walk, Konnory stayed close by his side.

"They are questioning much. Each meeting seems to turn into debates. They will figure it out – eventually. So much has happened in such a short amount of time. Our numbers are growing every day and we're still learning how to survive here without him. Debates such as you heard today happen frequently. Follow the King's laws or let them go? Someday, they will realize it isn't about the law but about the heart. Do we follow the King's laws to somehow attract his attention and find favor, or do we obey them out of love and honor for him?"

"That is the point exactly," Konnory said. "Why don't you tell them that?"

"I have - several times," James replied. "Jael told them as well. He would become so frustrated with them. Actually, with all of us, but he was patient. You will be the same, I expect."

"You speak to me as if we were old friends," Konnory said.

"Perhaps we are," James said. "I believe you are from the Kingdom?"

Konnory was taken aback. "You believe me to be not human?" he asked.

"Most certainly," James replied.

"And that doesn't bother you?"

James put his head back and laughed. "When you've grown up with the Prince of the Universe, nothing supernatural bothers you. If strange things weren't happening, then I would be bothered. Watchers coming and going, visitors from the Kingdom, they were all part of life with Jael.

As kids, we didn't see much, but we knew early on that he wasn't normal. How could he have been? We spent a lot of time by the sea and it would be in the early hours of the morning that he would talk of the Kingdom. At first, I thought he was just a crazy kid. It didn't take long before I realized there was something else going on, something much bigger than I." The two continued walking.

"He never really fit here. Not that he was odd – well, in a way he was odd. But there was always something distant in his eyes, as if he could see beyond our scope. The day that changed it all for me was the day they took him to the Temple and he began debating with the Temple Leaders. I had accompanied mother and father that day as well. It was amazing to hear him talk of our history and the true meaning of the Temple writings. This uneducated kid with little means holding his own with the Temple Leaders. I could listen to him for hours and did many times." James paused.

"He was a dear brother and friend. I was fortunate to have been a part of his life while he was here. I expect you know him as well as I."

"In some ways," Konnory said. "But in others, you have the advantage."

The two walked on in silence. A short distance later James arrived at his home. Stopping to ask Konnory to join him, the two entered the residence. James and Konnory spent the remainder of the afternoon together. They talked little of Jael, but more of the debate from earlier that day.

Konnory did not reveal who he was, that time would come. This afternoon they were simply brothers from the Kingdom. Just before dinnertime there was a knock at the door. James answered it with Konnory in tow.

Standing in the doorway was a young lad, face red from a mixture of excitement and sweat. Out of breath and wiping the dust that had begun accumulating on his face, he burst out, "There's been an arrest."

James shook his head, "Who this time?" he asked.

"Gad and Benjamin," the lad replied as he bent over in an attempt to catch his breath.

"What good deed have they done now?" James asked.

"You know that old crippled beggar that sits outside the Temple Gate?" the messenger began, still bent over and now pointing toward the Temple.

"Yes, I see him frequently. Don't tell me they did something horrible and gave him food on the Sabbath?" James asked.

"No, for that the Temple Leaders may have turned their eyes. Gad did much more than that. The man asked for money and Gad replied, 'Money have I none to give you, but what I do have I gladly offer.' With that he reached down, took the man's hands and brought him to his feet."

"He healed a crippled beggar and for that they have been arrested?" Konnory asked.

James looked at Konnory with raised brow. "Welcome to Turayn," he said. Turning his attention back to the messenger he asked, "Where is this man now? Did he refuse such a gift?"

"Actually, he followed Gad and Benjamin into the Temple as if he were a kid skipping along the path. He drew a lot of attention," the lad said in between gasps. "They've been taken for questioning. Most likely they have been locked up."

"We should go," James said. "I'm not sure what we can do or even if we will be able to see them, but it would be good to be close by. Are you going to join me?" he asked Konnory.

"Wouldn't miss it!" Konnory replied.

"We'll leave shortly," James informed the messenger, who simply nodded, turned, and ran off.

"Arrested for freeing that poor soul from his daily prison," James closed the door. "If they could only see how much good they prevent from happening here in Turayn."

"Remind me again which ones are Gad and Benjamin," Konnory said.

"Benjamin and Jael had a very close relationship, as did we all," James said. "But there was something different about

Benjamin, he saw thing differently. He lives on a..., how do I describe it? It's an emotional level that few understand."

"And Gad?" Konnory asked.

"And Gad." James paused for a moment. "Gad is quick to speak. It wouldn't be so bad if he spoke quietly, but no, not Gad. He speaks with great boldness."

"Is he the cock-a-doodle-doo boy?" Konnory blurted out with great excitement.

"The cock-a-what?" James inquires with a strange grin.
Konnory began to laugh. "Jael calls him the cock-a-doodle-doo boy. He is the one that was so quick to proclaim he would never denounce Jael, correct?"

"Yes..."

"Then before Jael was arrested he did, and not just once, but three times – correct?" Konnory asked.

"Correct...and then the rooster crowed and... cock-a- doodle-doo...I get it. Even during those horrific hours Jael speaks of such things," James said placing his hand on Konnory's shoulder. "Let's go see if we can assist. I doubt greatly that they will even let us get close."

Konnory and James headed out of the house and to the courtyard where such trials were held. As they approached,

102

they could see a rather large crowd of people. "I don't believe they have been put into confinement yet," James said.

As they drew closer, standing on the outer ring of those encircling the hearing, James continued, "I believe I can see Gad, there in the center." He turned to point Konnory in the right direction, but he was nowhere to be found. Unphased by the disappearance, James did his best to hear the conversation.

"They did what?" asked a man who appeared to be the Leader of the Temple Leaders.

"They are preaching in the name of Jael," was the response. "That is not allowed!" asked the Leader.

"And they healed a man!" said another. James recognized the voice. He strained to see. Pushing his way through the group, he got close enough to see the inner circle.

"Seems like a punishable deed to me. How dare anyone improve the life of another? This man was a cripple and should have remained as one." To James' surprise, the other leaders were nodding their heads. He focused in on the man who was speaking. He was tall and thin, and James was sure he wasn't one of the Temple leaders. He knew the voice, however. There was no doubt it was Konnory.

"They healed me!" exclaimed the healed beggar who was standing behind Gad and Benjamin. "They healed me in the name of the King!"

"How dare they do such a thing! We all know such acts of the Kingdom are punishable up to death," the tall man said.

"Yes, yes! He is correct!" added the other Temple leaders. James couldn't believe that they were so blind not to see a new stranger among them.

"But then again," the tall man held up his hand and the group silenced. "We cannot argue the point that this man was healed, for he stands here in front of us. I'm not sure if killing these men for doing an act of the Kingdom is wise." The tall one was now standing next to the Leader. He turned slightly as to speak directly to him, "Perhaps if we were to get rid of the man, something could be done." The Leader nodded slowly, considering the option. "Or if they had healed someone less visible, but who had entered the Temple gates without seeing this man. He is recognizable and is most certainly not going to keep quiet. Death nor prison would not be a good decision for you. It could put you in a bad light." With that, the Leader's expression changed. He was no longer thinking about Gad and Benjamin, but of himself.

"Punishment for speaking in the name of Jael, that's all. That should send the message," the tall one turned back to the group.

The other leaders began to mumble softly among themselves. James glanced at Gad and then back to the Leaders. The tall one was no longer there. Instinctively, James turned to his right, fully expecting to see Konnory standing next to him. He was not disappointed.

Konnory smirked. He was intrigued that neither his disappearance - nor reappearance - had seemed to affect James. "You have witnessed much, haven't you?" Konnory asked.

"Yes, my friend. Turayn life and Kingdom activity are blended together," James replied, as he turned his attention back to the center of the circle. "I've yet to see the Watchers and Warriors as Timothy did, but I have seen their endeavors. I live in a state of amazement, but not surprise. Never surprise."

"We are going to be good friends," Konnory said as he placed his hand on James' shoulder.

"Perhaps we will become brothers," James said.

Gad and Benjamin were flogged that day. Flogging was the best of the worst punishment. After they were released, James collected the two men and took them back to his home and tended to their wounds.

Konnory did not accompany them, and James did not speak of Konnory or his involvement in the decisions made that day. He hoped that he would meet Konnory once again. In his soul, he was sure their paths would cross.

9

It had all the makings of a war room. Maps, sketches, blueprints, and stacks of tablets were spread out across the massive table. Except for its location, it looked identical to the early days of The Plan.

Carasi, Ferrul and Konnory gathered at one end of the table. Waldemar, Magnor and Quaine controlled the rest of the table. So deep in conversation were all, none of them realized the King had entered. He quietly walked over to the table.

"Are these the final plans?" he asked.

"Hello Father," said a startled Carasi.

"I wish these were the final plans," Ferrul said, "there is a long way to go!"

"It is impossible to determine the size of the area we will need. Until we have that equation, we cannot determine the number of warriors required," Magnor said as he rubbed his forehead. He continued scanning the work from one end of the table to the other.

"Has there been any further word from the Messengers?" the King asked.

"They are making regular reports." Magnor continued, "It appears that Patho's message has been sounded loud and clear. It is difficult to find anyone willing to speak freely."

"Waldemar, what do we have from the commanders?" asked the King.

"The requests continue to increase. However, it appears they may be tapering off, but at the rate they were being received that doesn't equate to much." Waldemar reported. The King shook his head in disappointment.

"Is it possible to design the boundaries in a way that is expandable? We can't wait much longer," Quaine said. "If we began with what we think is sufficient and have the capability to expand the boundaries easily, it would allow for us to continually make adjustments. The ultimate hope is that we would be able to decrease the size in the future."

Ferrul instantly lit up, and Carasi scratched his head. "That is exactly what we need to do!" Carasi said as he pointed to the drawing. "We have been looking at this the same way we did in planning for Turayn. That was defined, this is not." Carasi was finding clarity as he spoke.

The room suddenly ignited in conversation once again. Ferrul and Carasi were throwing out numbers, measurements, and statistics. Magnor and Waldemar discussed the number of warriors required compared to the current regiments surrounding Turayn.

Quaine looked at the King, "I must report to Tayten," he said.

"I am sure he can do without you today," said the King. "Your insight is so very important."

"They can take it from here," Quaine said. "I do not want to leave Tayten shorthanded." Quaine turned and left the Throne Room. It was several minutes later when his absence was noted by the others.

"Where did Quaine go?" Ferrul asked.

"He felt he needed to check in with Tayten," the King replied.

"Tayten is not in need of his service," Ferrul said. "He spends more time with his guilt than with any of us. When is it going to stop?"

"Excuse me, sir," a voice interrupted. "I believe you should hear this." Standing at the end of the table were two figures - Odella and one of Magnor's captains.

"When did you get here?" Magnor directed his question to Odella.

"We arrived at the same time," Odella answered as she made her way to Magnor's side. "But we didn't come together. I came to check in on our mighty warriors."

Magnor smiled as he watched Odella walk around the table. The captain cleared his throat in hopes to regain Magnor's attention. "Yes, I'm sorry. You were saying..." Magnor said.

"As you are aware," the captain began, "We had twelve warriors volunteer to venture out into the Darkness. They were given strict instructions as to how long they should remain out there and exactly how far they should venture out. Nine of the men followed these instructions explicitly. Three took it upon themselves to go out further." Odella reached over and took Magnor's hand.

The captain continued, "All twelve have been under close observation since their return. The nine show signs of exhaustion, as was expected. They have recovered, but it took more time than what we had anticipated. The three," the captain paused. "The three are showing unusual signs."

"Are they ill?" Ferrul asked.

"No, it isn't that," the captain said. "They, too, experienced exhaustion. It took time for them to recover..."

"So, where is the issue?" Carasi asked.

"There appears to be a," he paused searching for the right description, "a deficiency of some type."

"A deficiency?" Magnor asked. "What do you mean?"

"Are they sick? What are the symptoms?" Ferrul scratched his head as he and Carasi shared glances of confusion.

"No one is able to pinpoint it exactly, or even describe it for that matter, but they are different. They feel the change but are unable to express what it is." Odella squeezed Magnor's hand tightly; she then let it go and walked out of the room.

"Stop all future excursions," Magnor said. "Until we can better understand what we are dealing with, we will put no one else in danger."

"Yes, sir. We anticipated that would be your response. All future excursions are on hold," said the captain.

"Where are the three now?" Waldemar asked.

"They are still under observation," replied the captain.

"Have they been home yet?" asked the King.

"No, Sire, we have not allowed them out of confinement," replied the captain.

"What are you thinking, Father?" Carasi asked. "Will that make a difference?"

"It may," answered the King. "This is new territory. No one had ever spent any extended length of time in the Darkness and returned to the Kingdom. We now know there are changes that happen after returning from Turayn."

"When Mother asked if anyone was aware of the effects the darkness could have, do you think this is what she may have seen?" Konnory asked.

"It may very well have been," the King replied. "Let them be with their loved ones. Have them select two who they want at their side. Watch closely, to see if it doesn't make a difference. Keep us updated."

"We will, Sire," the captain said as he saluted the King and took his leave.

Odella glided through the halls of the castle, making her way to the garden. She had barely made it out of the Throne Room before the tears began to flow. As she left the castle, she could hold back no longer. She dropped to the ground under an olive tree. The Queen had been walking through the garden on her way to the castle when she spotted her. As she grew closer, she heard the sobbing. She quietly approached and knelt down.

"What is it, my dear?" she asked softly.

"I can't let him go!" Odella replied. She attempted wiping her tears but was unable to stop their flow.

"Let who go?" the Queen asked ever so gently, sitting patiently, waiting for Odella to respond.

"Magnor. I can't...he can't...it will change him." Odella covered her face with her hands and cried.

The Queen stroked Odella's hair and gently moved it back away from her face. She then took Odella's hands in hers. They were trembling. The Queen held them and stroked them softly. She put her hand under Odella's chin and raised her head. "Now, tell me what this is all about," she said.

Odella took several deep breaths. She forced out every word. "The captain just reported that three warriors returned from the darkness and were... I don't know, he said there was a deficiency of some kind. No one seems to be able to explain it. But they are changed, they came back... different."

"What does that have to do with Magnor?" the Queen asked.

"I know Magnor, he won't allow his troops to go into the Darkness without taking part. He will be out there! He will be affected! What if Patho finds him? What if he doesn't come back? What if he comes back and he's...sick?" She began to shake. "I can't face that. It's all I can do to understand and accept the changes in me. I can't face him being changed...

because he is doing...good. What will I do?" Odella fell into the Queen's arms.

"Oh, my dear. What a horrible place the Darkness must have been. What fear must have tormented you in Turayn." She wrapped her arms around this fragile one. She began to gently rock her. The Queen pulled Odella's hair back, exposing her tear-soaked face and kissed her forehead. "Odella, you are home now," she whispered. "You are safe. There is no longer any reason to fear. My sweet child, the King and I have all the power needed to repair any damage done outside these gates. Konnory and Jael both experienced that healing power."

The Queens words found their way past Odella's tears and caught her attention. She took another deep, broken breath. Her body trembling, she looked up at the Queen. Was it possible? Was it possible that she and the King could remove any effects from time spent in the darkness? If it was, why hadn't they done so? Odella need not speak a word, the Queen was well aware of what she was thinking.

The soft gentleness of the Queen's touch had finally begun to break through Odella's fear. She brushed her hair back again and blotted her face. Odella's eyes were swollen and her cheeks red. "It wouldn't be wise for us to remove all the pain," she paused, "it is part of the healing process."

Odella's sobs were starting to be quieted. She once again attempted to dry her tear-soaked face with her sleeve and then she looked up at her Queen. Her smile warmed her. Her look comforted her. She felt like a child again. A child who was safe. A child who was loved. A child who had everything.

"Something allowed each of you to make the decision to leave. Each needs to discover why you chose to do so. That can only be done by remembering," the Queen said.

"But, Quaine?"

"Yes, my dear, Quaine. It is difficult for both the King and I to watch him suffer so. But we must. Quaine has to come to terms with what he did. He has to find a way to accept forgiveness. Nothing is accomplished by simply taking the pain away." Odella laid her head against the Queen's arm. "Magnor will be fine. There is nothing that can harm him. If he thought for a moment that he was hurting you...."

Odella sat up and wiped her face with both sleeves. "He isn't hurting me," she said. "I only fear because I know him so well. I know he is strong and honorable. I know his integrity will force him to be with his warriors."

"There is no need to worry, dear," the Queen said. She looked up to see Magnor standing at the castle entrance, scanning the gardens. "There is your strong warrior now." Odella turned to see him. "Go to him," the Queen said.

The Queen quickly brought Odella's attention back to her. She gently patted her face and smoothed her hair. Odella's petite features were puffy and red. There was no hiding it.

They stood, and Odella adjusted her garment. The Queen brushed off the olive leaves that had been their cushion.

As Odella turned away, the Queen reached down and took her hand. Odella turned back, "You are not to speak of this," she said gently, but with undeniable sternness. "No one knows." Odella's eyes opened wide.

"There will come a time that the Princes will come to understand the true power that is within them, but they must discover it on their own."

"Within them?" Odella asked.

"There is nothing that the King or I possess that doesn't also belong to the Sons," the Queen said. The two stood locked in each other's presence for what felt like an eternity. Odella felt her strength penetrate her fragile state; she warmed from her look. "Now go, Magnor is looking for you."

Odella turned to leave. With one step forward, she stopped and turned back to embrace the Queen.

"Thank you," she said ever so softly. "Thank you for everything."

The Queen held her tight. As Magnor began to make his way over, the Queen gently pushed Odella away and sent her off to meet her Prince.

10

ayten entered the Dining Room in order to make his final inspection before meeting with the head stewards. The conversation this morning had been very robust. Konnory and Jael were discussing Konnory's most recent visit to Turayn. Magnor, Odella, Carasi, and Ferrul were debating the actual number of warriors required to create a safe stronghold for the Fallen Souls. Each in the room fed off the others' energy and enthusiasm.

The King pushed back his chair and stood. Holding his hand out to the Queen, he said, "Shall we?"

The Queen took one final sip from her cup, pushed her chair back, and took the King's hand. Together they walked toward the doors. "Have a kingly day," Mother said as the King opened the door for her.

"And a Queenly one to you," Quaine said.

The temperature in the room instantly rose, but those in attendance froze. It was the first-time silence had filled the room all morning. The Queen turned back. She smiled graciously at Quaine. Her smile made her eyes wink. He returned the gesture. She looked around the room at the others. Sensing Carasi was on the verge of remarking to Quaine, she said "Have a good day, Carasi."

It was enough to distract him. "Yes, Mother, you as well," Carasi said. As the Queen passed through the doors, she caught the King's eye. He too was smiling as he watched her.

"With a few words and a smile, you control all of them," he whispered.

"It's what a true Queen does," she said, raising her brow. The Dining Room doors closed behind them.

"I'm off," Konnory announced as he pushed back his chair.

"Do you have an agenda for today?" Jael asked.

"Yes, of course. With Balbas involved, I am never without an agenda." Konnory flew his arms around, mimicking Balbas. "The Watchers are keeping us well-informed. There appears to be a Human that has caught the attention of more than one of them. I'm not sure you were aware of him while you were there. I don't have all the details, but this one looks like a real threat."

Konnory stood. "I am going to see your other brother today. I really like that guy!" he said. Jael smiled. "You know, James and I spend all our time talking about...," Konnory circled his fingers in the air and abruptly pointed them at Jael, "...you."

"I highly doubt that," Jael said with a laugh. "James is a good brother. I doubt that he would waste his time on such discussions."

"You do know him well," Konnory said. "Almost as if you were brothers," Konnory spun around on his heels and headed toward the door. He patted Jael on the shoulder as he passed.

"If he spends any more time with Balbas, we'll soon not be able to tell them apart," Jael remarked."

As Konnory entered Turayn he was met by what was quickly becoming a familiar group of Watchers. They accompanied him to James's home. Konnory knocked on the door but did not wait for an answer. Slowly opening it, he called "You here?"

"Yes, come on in. I was wondering when I would see you again," James said without looking up from his work.

Konnory walked into the room. "What has your attention?"

"It's a letter. I want to make sure I'm clear before I have it delivered."

"Is this intended for a special someone?"

"A few thousand special someone's," James responded. "Interested?"

"Would love to," Konnory said reaching out to take the paper.

> Consider it a great gift, friends, when tests and challenges come at you from all sides. You know that under pressure, your faith-life is forced into the open and shows its true colors. So don't try to get out of anything prematurely. Let it do its work so you become mature and well-developed, not deficient in any way.

> If you don't know what you're doing, ask the King. He loves to help. You'll get his help, and won't be condescended to when you ask for it. Ask boldly, believing, without a second thought. People who "worry their prayers" are like wind-whipped waves. Don't think you're going to get anything from the Master that way, adrift at sea, keep all your options open.

> When down-and-outers get a break, cheer! And when the arrogant rich are brought down to size, cheer! Prosperity is as short-lived as a wildflower, so don't ever count on it. You know that as soon as the sun rises, pouring down its scorching heat, the flower withers. Its petals wilt, and before you know it, that beautiful face is a barren stem. Well, that's a

picture of the "prosperous life." At the very moment everyone is looking on in admiration, it fades away to nothing.

Don't let anyone under pressure to give into evil say, "The King is trying to trip me up." The King is impervious to evil, and puts evil in no one's way. The temptation to give into evil comes from us and only us.

So, my very dear friends, don't get thrown off course. Every desirable and beneficial gift comes out of heaven. The gifts are rivers of light cascading down from the Father of Light. There is nothing deceitful in the King, nothing two-faced, nothing fickle. He brought us to life using the true Word, showing us off as the crown of all his creatures.

Konnory was interrupted by a young man busting through the front door. "At least I knocked," Konnory said defensively.

"You have to come quickly, its Amus! He is dead. Right there in front of everyone, he just dropped dead!"

"Calm yourself, my lad," James said. "Now tell me what happened."

"At the gathering, Amus came up to offer the money he got when he sold his land. As soon as he handed it over, he fell over dead. They are taking him out to bury him now. You have to come."

"Yes, we'll be right behind you," James said, as he turned the boy back toward the door and motioned for him to take the lead. "Coming?" he turned to ask Konnory.

"Right behind you."

The three wove through the streets to the place of the gathering. Gad was observing the burial. James approached him.

"What happened?" he inquired.

Gad looked shocked. He stood shaking his head in disbelief. "He brought the profits he claimed were from the sale of property. When asked if this was the price, he said it was. Something inside me knew it to be a lie. He had sold it for more. But that is not the real issue. He sold the property for more, claiming he would give it all away, thus he received a higher price. He kept back a portion for himself. It's not that he wasn't willing to give it all, it's that he lied in order to obtain a greater gain."

"Thinking he could manipulate the King," Konnory said. "I recall someone else who did such a thing."

"Does Sophie know?" James asked.

"I don't believe so," Gad replied.

"Let's get them back inside." James and Gad directed the group to return. They gave everyone time to calm down before they continued their meeting.

Konnory watched the door; it was a short time before Sophie entered. "Is that her?" he whispered to James. James nodded. "Let's see if they are two of a kind."

Sophie took a seat, and nervously looked around the room. Only able to remain seated for a few minutes, she stood and looked around as if to find her husband. She walked to the front to offer her profits to Gad. Gad hesitated. Then with clarity he asked, "Is this all the profits you and Amus made?"

"Yes, it is everything. We sold the property for the purpose of giving it away." Sophie said as she handed over the money.

"Why is it that you believe you can manipulate the King in such a way? Those who buried your husband a short time ago, will bury you also." The last word had barely left Gad's lips when Sophie fell to the ground – dead.

The very men who had just carried Amus out moments ago, covered Sophie and did the same. James and Konnory followed the processional but did not stay. They continued walking toward James' house.

"You should add this to your letter," Konnory said. "I would say we have all seen their true colors."

"I find myself so often apologizing to the King for the arrogance of the Human. It must grieve him so."

"Father is patient, but he is also just. He is well-aware of the arrogance of the Human," Konnory said.

"Father?" James questioned. "You say that the same way Jael spoke of him. May I assume you are brothers?"

"We are all brothers," Konnory replied. "We are all brothers from the Kingdom."

The two returned to James' home. As they sat discussing the issues that plagued Jael's followers, James paused, and Konnory noticed his demeanor change. Konnory could feel his concern.

"There is one," James began, "he's a young ruler that had caught my attention. He's wicked. It's the first time I think there may be nothing redeemable about him."

"There is always something redeemable," Konnory said. "For some, it just takes a while to find it."

"I'm not sure about this one. It will take all the powers of the Kingdom to get his attention."

"Well then, he will have all the power of the Kingdom. I will make sure of that," Konnory assured.

When Konnory returned to the kingdom, he went straight to the lower chambers. He was greeted by every attendant he passed, and to each he nodded in acknowledgment as they streamed by. Descending the final set of stairs, he stopped and scanned the room. Scouting the multiple groups of Watchers, Konnory finally spotted him in the middle of the room. Descending the final few steps, he forged his way through the crowd. It no longer took him time to adjust his vision. This place was not familiar to him.

"Sir," Balbas greeted, catching Konnory out of the corner of his eye. "We've just been discussing a young ruler in Taryn. He is trouble..."

"Yes! I was just there, and James was sharing with me. He feels it will take all the powers of the Kingdom to get his attention. There is great concern about this one," Konnory said.

"There should be," Balbas said as he directed Konnory over to a side table. "This one is going to be a challenge. James is right – all the powers of the Kingdom. He's smart, connected, and arrogant as – well, you know who. The Empire also has an eye on him. We're working on it. I've doubled the efforts."

"Triple them if need be," Konnory directed. "If he has the attention of the Watchers and the Humans, we need to act quickly."

"We can't be too quick with this one, Sir. As far as I can see, we have to nail it the first time. Any missed attempts will only make him angrier and more determined. We don't want that."

"No, no, we don't want to add to his fire. Tell me, do you believe we need Father's input?"

"Sir, that is your decision. We will continue our efforts here and if you feel the King needs to be included, his words are always welcome."

Konnory took a deep breath. "I'm confident you have this under control. I'll speak to Father and see if he can offer insight." Konnory reached out his hand and Balbas grasped it. "Thank you, my friend. I have full confidence that together we will not only stop this one, but we will successfully regain him for the Kingdom."

"We have already claimed him for the Kingdom," Balbas said as he looked around at the Watchers. "Now we just need to figure out how." Balbas smiled as Konnory broke into laughter.

"All the powers of the Kingdom!" Konnory said. "He'll never see us coming,"

Balbas stood eagerly, rubbing his hands together. "Oh sir, those are powerful words. I don't believe we need the King's input after all. This is our battle and *we have all the power of the Kingdom!*"

11

Carasi headed up to Quaine's chambers in hopes of bringing him up to speed on Magnor's battle. Quaine had not made himself available to join any of the recent planning sessions. When asked for his input, he would decline comment. Carasi was at the end of his patience. This was his final attempt to include Quaine in the battle plans.

As he climbed the stairwell, he felt less than hopeful. He knew if Quaine wasn't invested in the mission, it would be a liability. He knocked on Quaine's door, but there was no answer. He knocked again and shouted, "I know you are in there, we need to talk!" The door opened slowly. Carasi entered the room.

Waldemar came around the corner a short time later to see Carasi's exit and hear him yell back, "Do you not realize that by not accepting this forgiveness you are putting yourself and your guilt above Jael's sacrifice? I say brother, you are not worth that!" Carasi slammed Quaine's chamber door. Waldemar's presence took him by surprise. "See what you can do. I'm finished with him." Carasi headed toward the stairs and let out a loud, frustrated shout as he descended.

Tayten had heard the commotion and rushed to the scene. As Waldemar looked on, Tayten knocked on the door. There was no answer. Tayten looked at Waldemar as if looking for instruction.

"I don't know," Waldemar responded. "Try again." Tayten did just that. Again, there was no response. Tayten reached for the handle. "Don't!" Waldemar commanded. Tayten jumped back, startled by the command. "Sorry, I didn't mean to be so forceful. I'll see what I can do."

Waldemar took a very deep breath. In fact, he took two very deep breaths. Whatever was behind those doors could not be good. He closed his eyes and took a step closer to the door. He reached out his hand and knocked twice. There was no answer. With one more knock, Waldemar announced, "I'm coming in."

He reached for the handle, expecting for the door to be locked, but it was not. He opened the door slowly. The room was quiet and dark. He was sure Quaine was there, somewhere. He scanned the room; there standing in front of the far window was the motionless figure. He had no color in his face. His eyes were glazed; it seemed that he was unaware of Waldemar's presence. Waldemar walked to his side. The two stood, peering out into the gardens.

"She did a beautiful job, didn't she?" Quaine asked.

"You mean Odella? Yes, she did." Waldemar replied. There was a long silence.

"How do you do it?" Quaine asked without moving his focus.

"Do what?" replied Waldemar.

"How do you spend each day facing the King and Jael?" Quaine stood solemn.

Waldemar thought for a moment. He had never pondered this. Perhaps it was because the King himself had ushered him back into the Kingdom. Perhaps it was because he was much older than Quaine. Or, perhaps it was the simple fact that Waldemar was reminded daily of the King's grace and forgiveness, and that all he ever wanted to do was serve him every day.

Waldemar cleared his throat and gently said, "With a grateful heart, I suppose."

Quaine looked at Waldemar with a scowl. "A grateful heart? Isn't that a bit childish? After all they have done? After all we did?" There was anger in his reply. Quaine turned his focus back to the gardens.

"I guess it could appear that way," Waldemar replied. "But there is nothing childish about it. It takes every ounce of my being to keep my heart grateful." Waldemar turned and walked over to a large chair sitting in front of the fireplace. "And actually, you are correct," he continued, "Children are the only ones who seem to be able to give and receive forgiveness effortlessly.

"That is only because they don't understand the cost!" Quaine snapped.

"Perhaps," Waldemar replied. "But you do, don't you?"

"Yes, unfortunately I do." Quaine turned from the window. "I'm leaving," he said as he marched over to the bookcase.

"Leaving? To go where?" Waldemar responded very much in control, even though his emotions were wreaking havoc within him.

There was a very long pause, "Anywhere but in the Kingdom."

"So you're going to join Patho once again?" Waldemar questioned.

Quaine spun around. "NO! I would never do that!" he snapped.

"I don't believe there is any other choice. If you choose to leave the Kingdom this time, there will be no return. From what I can see, you will be making your point very clear."

"And what point is that?" Quaine asked.

"The one you have been trying to prove since you returned. That somehow you see yourself as better than Jael. That you were not part of The Plan. That you are above even the King." Waldemar spoke with great authority. His assertiveness surprised even himself.

"You are mad! That is not the reason." he replied. He began gathering his things.

Waldemar stood tall. He folded his arms, "Really? You leave the King once, and then you are the one who is pleading for forgiveness. Your Father and brothers work diligently to provide a way for you to return. You are given the privilege to participate in this plan, trusted to play a most important role. You are returned quickly to the Kingdom, due to two other brothers' impatience to get you home. You are welcomed into the Kingdom, into the King's presence without reserve. With great concern and love, you are placed under the love and guidance of your oldest friend, but YOU can't seem to forgive yourself."

Quaine began to respond, but Waldemar stopped him. "I'm not finished! You walked out the first time deceived. You leave again, and it will be out of your own Free Will. You will be declaring to all that Quaine, the son of the King of the Universe, is superior to his brother's sacrifice. You will be joining Patho for eternity whether you intend to or not!" Waldemar did not move, he stared at Quaine waiting for a response.

Anger boiled up within Quaine. He began moving toward the door. His walk was unsteady, bumping into the corner of the bed and tripping over the footstool. As he reached the handle, Waldemar said in a tone he had not used since he was in command of the Kings army's, "Goodbye then, I'll tell the King you left with a grateful heart!"

Quaine squeezed the handle. There was another long silence, neither one moved. Quaine dropped his head. "I could never deserve what he did for me," he whispered.

Waldemar remained steadfast. He hoped that Quaine was breaking. Finally, he took a step and made his way over to the door. Putting his arms on Quaine's shoulders, he said in a gentle tone, "None of us are or will ever be."

Quaine turned. He looked up at Waldemar. Waldemar saw the pain in his expression. He opened his arms and Quaine collapsed into him.

Waldemar wrapped his arms around him and felt him trembling. "There is not one who is worthy of such an act. There will never be one who can work to deserve such forgiveness. It is a simple choice. We choose to be either proud - or grateful." Waldemar squeezed Quaine a bit tighter. "I choose to be grateful," Waldemar said soberly. Standing there with Quaine resting against his chest, Waldemar gave him all the time he needed.

"I am so very guilty," Quaine finally whispered.

"Yes, you are!" Waldemar's response startled Quaine. He pulled back and looked up. Waldemar continued, "Guilt should never be thought of as a feeling, it's simply a fact. And yes, my son, you are extremely guilty...and so am I."

"Are you making light of this?" Quaine asked.

"In no way!" Waldemar responded. "The fact is - we are guilty. The greater fact is, that we are forgiven. I choose each day to be grateful for that forgiveness, knowing very well that I am guilty."

Waldemar pulled Quaine close. He felt a spark of joy ignite deep within his own soul. He understood Quaine's resistance. But possibly for the first time since his return, Waldemar felt a release within himself. He spoke the words again, "We are guilty. We are forgiven."

It was like a flame touching the dry brittle tips of kindling. It burns quietly and then suddenly the flame increases and spreads up until all is consumed. Waldemar could do nothing to restrain the flame. He felt it consume him and wished desperately that Quaine would feel its warmth. He began to smile. The smile quickly turned into a gentle laugh; it was filled with glorious release of joy. To Quaine's resistance, it was a contagious laugh.

Waldemar squeezed Quaine again. He put his head back and announced, "I am guilty. I am forgiven!" Waldemar was reaching a new height of acceptance. Any guilt that he may still have been carrying was breaking apart and falling off of him like broken chains.

Quaine felt it. It was impossible not to. "I am guilty. I am forgiven!" Quaine whispered. There was no joy in his tone.

Waldemar held him securely. He joined him in a whisper. "I am guilty. I AM forgiven!" they said in unison.

Waldemar felt his weakness. He thought that if he loosened his hold, Quaine would simply sink down to the floor. He whispered it once again, "I am guilty. I am forgiven."

Quaine knew the moment he walked through those gates that he had made a mistake. During his time in the darkness, he was consumed with getting word back to the King. There was no time after his realization who Jael was to contemplate anything, except for the task that he had agreed to take on. Then, suddenly he was home. He had felt nothing but guilt since his return. He had not allowed himself to see forgiveness. Carasi was correct in his accusation, he was stuck in his guilt.

Once again Quaine whispered, "I am guilty. I am forgiven." Waldemar was right. Guilt isn't a feeling. It is a fact. "And in my case, it's a real fact," Quaine said audibly. It made Waldemar smile.

Quaine repeated it over and over. Each time he said it, a weight was lifted from his shoulders. Each time he said it, he spoke with more confidence. He hadn't realized that each time he spoke it, he was growing louder in his delivery. He also grew stronger in his demeanor.

Finally breaking away from Waldemar's hold, he leaned his head back, and with outstretched arms shouted, "I AM guilty! I AM FORGIVEN!" The sheer volume startled both men.

Quaine walked over to the side of the bed and sat down with his head bowed, the details of his life replaying in his mind. He recalled the day in Turayn when he realized who he was. He relived the day Jael told him of The Plan. 'I do it for you' were Jael's words. "He did it for me," Quaine said out loud.

"I believe you've forgotten the rest of your conversation. Jael was relentless in pursuing The Plan - his willingness to become the final sacrifice, that he did for all who had left. You gave him a reason to go, but he chose to become the final sacrifice," Waldemar said walking over to Quaine's side.

"I am guilty. I am guilty," Quaine said once again.

"Most certainly," Waldemar responded.

Quaine fell back on the bed. Looking to the ceiling, he again repeated the words over and over. For the first time, those three words had meaning. They took root in his soul and began to grow deep within him. "I am forgiven of so very much."

"Yes, you are," reassured Waldemar. "But your Father's forgiveness is so much greater than your guilt. How could you ever think it would not be enough?"

Waldemar took a seat next to him, "Quaine, when you focus on your guilt, you are focused on you; when you see forgiveness, you see your Father."

Tears began to flow from Quaine's eyes. They ran down the side of his face and onto the bed. Waldemar waited patiently. He knew each tear was washing Quaine clean. After a long silence, Quaine sat up. Looking at Waldemar, he said one final time, "I am guilty, I am forgiven!"

He began to smile. Joy and contentment began to take hold. His eyes cleared. This new revelation seemed to permeate every ounce of his being. As Waldemar watched, Quaine was taking on a new appearance. There was a sharpness in his eyes, a glow in his smile. Each felt the heaviness of the room began to dissipate.

Then suddenly, he burst into laughter and tears. Quaine stood, and taking Waldemar's hands, he pulled him to his feet. They began to dance around the room. After a few moments, and just as many awkward steps, Waldemar suggested, "Let's go see Jael."

Quaine stopped and hesitated. "I am guilty, I am forgiven!" he whispered. Looking up at Waldemar, he said, "Yes, let's go see Jael, and I believe I need to speak to Father as well." They made their way to the door and Quaine reached for the handle. He stopped. He turned toward Waldemar, "Thank you my friend. Thank you."

"My sincere pleasure, my son." Waldemar put his hand on Quaine's shoulder and gave it a squeeze. "Guilt is not a feeling, it's a fact."

Quaine nodded and unlatched the door. As he opened it, there appeared to be great commotion in the hall as the seven individuals who had been smashed up against it clumsily dispersed.

"What are you all doing?" Quaine asked.

"Well..." began Konnory, rubbing his forehead and looking at the floor.

"We heard shouting!" explained Ferrul.

"Yes...yes we did!" added Tayten, failing miserably at appearing confident in his answer.

The King stepped forward, "Quaine, we are all very.."

"Stop Father. You don't have to say it. Waldemar and I have had a very long discussion. I see it all very clearly, or at least as clear as I have since I returned."

"We should have never asked you..." Jael began.

"No! No! don't ever say that! It was an honor that you trusted me enough to be a part of The Plan – a plan that I pleaded with you to create." Quaine responded. "I have been foolish, not childish as Waldemar has pointed out so well. I have been proud, and once again I find myself asking for forgiveness." Quaine looked up at the King.

"You are forgiven," offered the King.

Quaine looked back at Waldemar and smiled. Turning his attention to Father he said, "I am so very grateful!" For those in attendance they watched as Quaine began to radiate.

Then in an instant, he was engulfed by his five brothers. They surrounded him as they headed down the hall toward the stairs. The King stood with Waldemar and Tayten.

"What did you say?" Tayten asked. At that moment they heard Quaine shout as he descended the stairwell, "FORGIVEN!"

The three laughed. The King looked at Waldemar waiting for a response. "I simply said that guilt was not a feeling, it was a fact."

"Brilliant! Brilliant!!" said the King. "Soon you'll be ready to..."

"Oh, Sire. No. No to whatever it is! I am pleased to be here, with you and the Princes. I need nothing more!" Waldemar said with a new-found confidence.

"All right. You may stay awhile longer." The King put his hand on Waldemar's shoulder. "I wouldn't want you any other place."

Waldemar replied, "I am grateful!"

12

"**J**ames asked me on the first visit if we were brothers," Konnory said, as he and Jael walked down the hall. "Did you answer?"

"No, not as he expected. I said we were all brothers from the Kingdom."

"Ah, he's figured you out already. He was always the clever one. It's good to see they are putting such men as their leaders. I have no doubt he is compassionate in all his dealings."

Konnory put his hand on Jael's shoulder. "I know how much you desire to join me."

Jael smiled in a way that made his eyes twinkle. "I am there always," he said. The two walked to the entrance of the castle, where Jael stopped and Konnory continued on.

As was becoming his usual visit, Konnory was taken to James' home. He knocked but did not wait for an answer. "You in?" he asked as he entered the front door.

"You know very well I'm in," James replied. "You wouldn't be here if I wasn't."

Konnory laughed. "Still writing?"

"Always. They need continual encouragement and guidance. Jael understood that. I get weary of it at times, but all I need is to think of him and I move on. He must have been weary of us regularly, but he never showed it."

"Can I read it?"

"Yes, but first we have another visit to make. Seems every time you are here someone is arrested or drops dead. I'm not sure if they happen because you are here, or you are here because they have happened."

"Where are we headed this time, to the grave or jail?"

"Jail. They've been arrested again."

"The same two?"

"Yes."

"Now what good have they done?"

"Teaching Jael's words in the courtyard. They were arrested and now sit in jail."

"But it's late. Soon it will be dark. Let's wait a bit. It will look differently in the morning." Konnory said with a suspicious grin.

James stared at him for a moment. He had heard Jael say the same many times. "I'll trust your judgment - this time. Would you like to join me for dinner?" James asked.

"I would be delighted. A real dinner in Turayn, I've not partaken in a real meal...," Konnory abruptly stopped talking. James did not need to know that sitting across from him was the first Human to enter Turayn. Brothers with Jael, he may be able to understand. The first man? Konnory wasn't willing to press it.

Dinner was served and sleeping arrangements made. During the middle of the night, when all were fast asleep, Konnory enlisted the assistance of the Watchers. "Take me to the jail where they are imprisoned."

In a matter of minutes, Konnory stood outside the prison. It was heavily guarded. "It appears that there is no way in," he said. The Watchers chuckled, which in turn made Konnory do the same. He loved to hear their delight. It was a sound he could never imagine tiring of. "Let's go," he finally instructed.

Instantly, Konnory was standing in front of the locked prison doors. Those inside its confines were still awake. They sat on the ground arm in arm humming. The melody was similar to one child learn in the Kingdom. Konnory joined in. It wasn't until the prisoners stopped and Konnory continued on that they realized they had a guest.

"Don't be afraid," Konnory said. "It's time to leave."

None of those transported that night could explain how it happened. All they knew was that one moment they were locked inside, and the next they were standing in the very courtyard where they had been arrested. To their further surprise, a meal was waiting for them. And just as abruptly as they had been transported, Konnory had disappeared.

As morning dawned, James found Konnory reading his latest letter.

> Listen, dear friends. Isn't it clear by now that the King operates quite differently? He chose the world's down-and-out as the Kingdom's first citizens, with full rights and privileges. This Kingdom is promised to anyone.

"It's good," Konnory offered. "I trust they are taking heed?" Konnory put down the papers. "Seems I have another appointment with a few Temple Leaders," he said with a grin James was becoming very familiar with.

"Would this have anything to do with those we left in jail last night?" James asked.

"Quite possibly. To get you caught up, they aren't in jail this morning. You'll find them in the courtyard. I believe they are continuing where they left off yesterday."

Now James expression mirrored that of Konnory's. His mind raced back over times when the unexplained happened and Jael's only response was to shrug his shoulders, and with wide open eyes and a grin of pure joy, let him know that all was well.

"This I want to see," James said. "May I join you?"

"I have a meeting to attend first. Make your way to the courtyard."

With those simple instructions, Konnory left. James changed his clothes hastily. He headed for the courtyard where he did, indeed, find the same men teaching Jael's words who were arrested the day before. "Surely the King's ways are different than ours," he said to himself.

Konnory entered the counsel room as the Counsel Leaders awaited the arrival of the prisoners. When the guards returned, they were empty handed.

"Where are the prisoners?"

"They were not there?" the captain reported.

"What do you mean, not there? They were there last night. We all witnessed it. How have they escaped?"

"The prison remains secure. No lock is missing or has been tampered with. It is as secure as it was when we left them there yesterday."

"What do the guards say?"

"They are perplexed as we. There was no sound or commotion reported during the night. They claim they heard them singing well into the night. There is no way out except through the gates and those are all securely locked."

"You'll find these prisoners back in the courtyard. I saw them there on my way here." Once again Konnory had made himself a contributing part of the conversation.

The room was no longer quiet. "Go arrest them at once!" commanded the Temple leader.

"...or again," Konnory said under his breath.

A short time later, the men were standing in front of the counsel. Unwilling to bring up the matter that they had somehow escaped, the leader focused on their preaching, rather than their mysterious disappearance.

"You were instructed not to teach the lessons of Jael," he orders.

"We will choose to obey the King," Gad said boldly. "You put Jael to death, but it was the true King who brought him back to life. We will obey his words and his teachings."

"Gad," Konnory said softly. "You are a bold one."

"And you can join Jael," the Leader said. "Put them to death!" Konnory nudged the man next to him. "Are you going to speak up, or should I?" The man looked at Konnory. How did he know he wanted to stop this? How did he know he was on the verge of speaking up? "Go on then," Konnory said.

The man stood, "Council, if I may. I would suggest that death is not the appropriate penalty for these men's acts. Their followers are great and increasing in number. Death for speaking Jael's teachings could easily cause even greater attention to their teachings." The Council listened earnestly.

Konnory leaned over, "Well done, not sure if I could have done better myself." The man looked questioningly at Konnory as he returned to his seat.

After more discussion, the Council took the advice and removed the death penalty. The men were once again flogged, warned sternly not to speak of Jael again, and released. James was there to take them home and attend to their wounds.

Konnory caught up with them as they journeyed through the dirt roads. "I'm not sure how you did it," James said.

"The King operates quite differently," Konnory said. "I believe I read something like that this very morning."

James smiled and nodded. "I wish we had been able to save Stephen." Konnory noticed the immediate change in James as he spoke. "He was so young. With more time, he could have had great influence," James said.

The men entered the house. James had his attendants take the newly released prisoners to be tended to. Konnory escorted James to a small courtyard in the rear of the house. "Tell me about this Stephen," Konnory said.

"I was there when it happened. He was teaching the grace and faith that Jael taught. They must have been waiting, the arrest happened so very quickly. During the trial the next morning, that kid was magnificent. He spoke with great authority, reminding me of Jael as he spoke. It surprised me that he was allowed to say as much as he did. He started back at the beginning of time. He spoke of Haddad and Jair. He quoted the Temple Writings. I think they were surprised at his knowledge. It wasn't until he compared them to their forefathers, calling them stiff-necked and sinful, that's when the anger erupted."

"It wasn't his words that had my attention," James continued. "It was his appearance. As he spoke, something about him began to change. He looked - well almost as if he were already back in the Kingdom. There was such peace, such joy, such contentment. I couldn't take my eyes off of him.

"They dragged him out into the streets yelling and chanting. I kept my eyes on the lad, I couldn't take them off. There was a moment when he looked heavenward, it seemed he was looking up, but he was not seeing Turayn." James paused, he too was now looking heavenward. Konnory waited. "He mumbled something, I couldn't make it out. There was a young boy standing close to him, I pulled him back and asked if he had heard what was said. The boy hesitated for a moment and replied, 'I see him. He is standing with his arms outstretched waiting for me to come home.' I think he's already gone mad!"

Konnory remembered this day vividly. As James told the story, Konnory recalled sitting with Jael. As James told of the young man looking up, Konnory recalled Jael reaching his hands downward as if to pick up a child. His eyes focused as he mouthed, "keep your eyes on me." Konnory had been there. He had witnessed it all, just from a different vantage point.

James continued, "He looked as if nothing around him existed; as if he was already in the Kingdom."

James paused once again. "There was a young ruler in the crowd," James' tone moved from compassion to anger. "When the guards removed Stephen's blood-soaked robe, they threw it and it landed at this ruler's feet. He stood so proud, so pompous, so pleased - as if it were his accomplishment."

Konnory reached out and took James' arm. "He is in the Kingdom now," Konnory said. "I can assure you that his homecoming was celebrated." Konnory's encouragement broke the heaviness that covered the two.

"Yes, he is home now. Something we can all look forward to," James said. "That young ruler who stood watching. He is the same we spoke of last time. He is strong, a strong and evil force. He is just beginning his conquests, but he is pursuing Jael's followers with a vengeance. He's one to watch. He could be a true threat and cause great harm to Jael's purpose."

"You are right," Konnory said. "We've been aware of his ability to gain power in such a short time. The Watchers are on guard and keeping the Kingdom informed. You are right to be worried, he has the power to do great damage."

"Do you know what you will do with him?" James asked.

"Not yet, but we are aware. His time is not far away," Konnory said. Once again that grin that James was becoming more and more familiar with began to appear.

"Please let me be present for that one," James said.

"If it's within my power to do so, sir, you will have front row seats!"

13

Patho's supposed torment could only be speculated upon. The Messengers and Transporters had been unable to detect what exactly Patho was doing.

The requests to remove the original request from the Fallen Souls continued to come in. What was more discouraging was the realization that the requests for forgiveness had also dwindled. It baffled the Princes and Balbas that even those lost in the vast Darkness could be controlled by fear. One would have thought that when one finds themselves at the end of all hope, fear would not have control. What they had not understood was that fear was what held them in their hopelessness.

The holding area to protect the Fallen Souls from whatever it was that Patho was doing had been designed. Although the goal was to protect the Fallen Souls, first priority was to protect any of the warriors who would be standing guard. They were exploring new and unknown territory. No one knew for sure what effects being out in the Darkness for any length of time could have.

Out in the Vast Darkness, the Messengers and Transporters continued to spread the word that protection for those seeking redemption was coming. The news brought a seed of hope. When hope and fear sit on either side of the stick, the only one to decide the victor is the one holding the stick.

As Quaine had suggested, the holding area was designed to expand, and contract, as needed. This would be accomplished by increasing or decreasing the number of warriors who created its boundaries.

Magnor had been pleased by the number of warriors who volunteered for this mission. As each was interviewed, it was clear they all had a common purpose. For each had a family member or friend who had not yet returned to the Kingdom.

Magnor and Carasi had underestimated the number of new recruits wanting to serve in this new mission. Many were Fallen Souls who had returned to the Kingdom. This required the two brothers to evaluate the current training process. After great debate, it was decided that new recruits would be divided into two groups: recruits and redeemed recruits. The next questions was who would train the redeemed recruits.

"We can try to include them in the regular training," Carasi said.

"That could be a great risk," Ferrul said. "Do we wait until they have completed their proving time?"

"That would be best," answered Carasi.

"Then you are talking unmeasurable inconsistency in our timing. No two proving times are equal," Ferrul said.

Magnor had been pacing as he evaluated his brother's words. "You are right," said he. "We cannot take away from the regiments assigned to Turayn. In fact, we need to fortify them. I have no issue with rotating new recruits there. But we cannot risk Turayn's safety for any reason."

"Exactly," Carasi said. "It would be foolish to weaken that protection to provide a safe confine for the Fallen Souls who haven't gotten there yet."

"So, our only real issue is training the redeemed recruits?" the Queen asked.

"Yes," Carasi answered.

The Queen looked at Quaine and Waldemar and smiled. It was a look that warmed Quaine and sent a chill down Waldemar's neck. "I believe the answer is sitting at this table," she said. Waldemar shifted in his chair. Quaine rubbed his forehead.

The King lit up with childish excitement. "I believe you are correct," he said.

"Of course!" Magnor said as he stomped his foot and pointed at the two men. "Of course! You would be the best for the job. You will know immediately when the new recruits are ready. You'll understand what each will need and who will need additional time. Mother, you are brilliant!" Magnor stood behind Carasi, reaching out to slap him on the back of the head, but Carasi dodged just in time. Why didn't you think of it?"

"She outdoes me most of the time!" Carasi agreed. "I had always thought my brilliance...," Ferrul let out a burst of laughter. Carasi looked sternly at him and continued, "...I had thought my BRILLIANCE came from Father, but I'm beginning to wonder."

"Excuse Me?" the King responded. Those seated at the table did not hold in their amusement.

"Back to the issue at hand," Magnor said, attempting to regain control. "Waldemar, Quaine, we need you to clear your responsibilities. Tayten will find a replacement for Quaine, and Waldemar, we need someone to take on your responsibilities."

"What is it that you do?" Ferrul replied jokingly, making Waldemar blush ever so slightly.

"Konnory and Jael are out of the question; their focus is Turayn." Carasi said, "Ferrul, I know you don't have any extra time. Who else do we have to draw from?"

"Tayten will have no problem finding replacements to assume your responsibilities here in the castle. But it's the interaction you have with the commanders that is delicate." Waldemar was frantically scrolling through his head for words he could use to get him out of this.

"Isn't it time that Odella comes in from the gardens?" the Queen asked softly. The room was once again quiet. Magnor began to nod his head slowly.

"Yes, Mother, I do believe it is time," Magnor replied. "And it would be a perfect responsibility for her. It would allow us to be working together again." The Queen recognized Magnor's expression of delight. Magnor was definitely his Father's son. "I will ask her this afternoon. So that settles it, we all have our orders."

"Wait!" Waldemar said louder and bolder than he had anticipated. He placed his hand over his heart, "I greatly appreciate your confidence in me, or us, but I'm not sure I fully understand what you are asking."

"I believe we have just been assigned the task to create and initiate a training program for the new redeemed recruits," Quaine said. "A program that provides each a proving time, while training as a warrior."

Magnor nodded his head. "That is exactly what you have been assigned." Giving Waldemar his full attention he continued, "Do you have any objections..."

Ferrul interrupted, "Let me clarify that. Do you have any objections we would agree with?" Waldemar sat back in his chair; he knew there were no words that would get him out of this one.

Carasi stood and took control of the room. "Waldemar and Quaine, let's take a short break and when we re-adjourn, we will be laying out the training for the redeemed recruits. Magnor, it appears that we have enough troops to set this mission in motion. We still need to name this mission..." Carasi shook his head. "I really don't like Holding Place, but it will do for now."

"Perhaps Mother has a suggestion for a name," Ferrul said in a condescending tone.

The Queen rose from her chair and walked toward Carasi. Standing behind him, she put her hands on his shoulders and said, "Don't let them get to you; they could not do any of this without you." She kissed the back of his head. "There was a time I could outdo you, but not anymore." She gently patted his shoulder. "What do you think about Stronghold?"

Carasi began to laugh, "It's perfect!" he replied.

Magnor and his captains set out to begin establishing the Stronghold. Troops were deployed slowly; each making it to the edge of the Kingdom in a manageable rotation, not to overpower the local villages. The holding area was opposite Turayn, sandwiching the Kingdom between them. On one

side were those waiting to enter Turayn. On the other was
Turayn.

On the decided day, Magnor stood at the edge of the Kingdom
looking out into the Darkness. He couldn't help but recall the
first time he found himself in this position. On that day, he
stood with Father and his brothers as they began creating the
place that would allow the Fallen Souls to return home. That
now seemed like a lifetime ago.

The King had held to his word, this was Magnor's battle. On
this day, he was surrounded by his captains and commanders
as they ventured to create a place of protection for those
who desired to come home. The first regiment was trained
and ready. As they reported for duty, Magnor was there to
support and acknowledge their willingness to serve. Lined up
in pairs, the first two warriors took one step into the Darkness.
The two turned and stood face to face leaving enough room
between them for another pair to walk. The next took their
first step and walked between the first, then they turned and
stood shoulder to shoulder.

With the addition of each pair of warriors, the protected
walkway grew.

When half the of the circumference of the Stronghold was
established, Magnor made his way through the warrior-lined
walkway. As he passed each warrior he saluted, stopping
frequently to thank them for their service.

It was now time to complete the process. From the line of those who made up the inner wall, the first turned and walked through the formation to the end. Magnor watched as the doubled-lined walkway became a strong, defined boundary. The warriors stood at attention, leaving no gaps between them.

Because of Quaine's suggestion to create a boundary that could increase and decrease, one warrior was to be positioned in front of and between every third warrior. This provided an immediate ability to increase the boundaries by simply stepping onto the line. The boundaries could increase by one third in an instant.

By the time the wall of warriors was complete, it was time to begin rotation. The replacement regiment was to enter from the inside of the boundary. Each warrior would stand in front of and between those they were replacing. On a single command, the replacements would step back as those they were replacing stepped forward. It was an instant exchange. At no time was any warrior allowed to be on the exterior of the Stronghold. Their power and protection came from being connected to each other. Stepping outside of this protection would put everyone at risk.

Unlike the warriors guarding Turayn, who had the Darkness behind them and Turayn in front of them, those guarding the Stronghold would have the Darkness both behind them and in front of them. There still remained great question as to what effects this could have on each warrior. The threat of experiencing the deficiency reported earlier still remained.

It took only moments from the time the boundaries of the Stronghold were secure for the first of the Fallen Souls to make their way in. They were informed they would risk being removed if they spoke with the warriors. There could not be any interaction of any kind. Each warrior stood strong and secure, no easy task as each was wondering, hoping, and trusting that one of these Fallen Souls represented a family member or friend who had not yet returned.

Magnor made regular trips to check on the troops. He, too, underestimated the emotional effect it had on him. He could not help but think that if Odella had not already returned home, she would have been one of these. If Quaine was still lost, he would have been here, not training future warriors. It was likely that Palti was here, somewhere in this mass.

Upon Magnor's return home from each of his visits, Odella observed him closely. She felt he was changing, but she would not say it was a deficiency. Magnor's compassion for the Fallen Souls was deepening. There were no signs of deficiency, rather, with each journey to the Stronghold, he was increasing in character.

14

Abaddon entered the Pit reluctantly. Patho had called this meeting. It was not clear what was to be discussed, but Abaddon assumed they would be continuing discussion of the attempt to stop any Fallen Soul from submitting a request. He had seen Serpent as he was leaving Turayn, who instructed him to inform Patho he would be late. Abaddon knew what Patho's reaction would be. It didn't matter that he was simply the messenger. He would be the one to absorb Patho's wrath.

Sam, Syrus, and Sul had also been summoned. Since the last meeting, these three had been put in charge of finding their own recruits willing to assist Patho. They had been somewhat successful, but not everyone was willing to join in the battle, those that were, were a repulsive group.

Patho insisted that the new recruits not be invited. He wanted as little interaction with the Fallen Souls as possible. They were simply a means to an end. He didn't need to see them, talk with them, or interact in any way.

"I call this meeting to order," Secretary said. Sam, Syrus, and Sul crouched down on the ground. As each dropped, a cloud of soot billowed out from underneath them. Abaddon chose to sit between Secretary and Sam. He felt they may come in handy as a shield if, or rather when, Patho decided to hurl something his way.

"Where's Serpent?" Patho screeched. No one reacted. "*Idiots!*" he shouted as he glared at Abaddon.

Abaddon sat silently. He can deliver his own messages, he thought looking at Patho, ready for whatever Patho may throw at him. He did prefer actual items rather than his anger, objects he could dodge, and today he had two shields sitting on either side.

"He's becoming much too arrogant," Patho snapped.

"Becoming?" Secretary asked. Patho jerked his attention away from Abaddon. Abaddon had no idea why Secretary survived Patho's daily attacks. "Let's get started," Secretary said, ignoring Patho's stare. "I understand that you have new recruits."

Sam, Syrus, and Sul nodded in unison. Syrus spoke up, not wanting to give Patho any chance to respond, "Yes, we have. And our numbers are increasing." Syrus was nodding his head as he looked at his cohorts who joined in the affirmation. "They are eager to assist in any way needed."

"They aren't coming?" Patho interjected.

"No." Sul answered, hesitating afterward. He was sure they had received strict orders not to bring anyone else. He was sure before they entered, but once in Patho's presence, it was difficult to remain sure of anything.

"They were not instructed to attend," Syrus said. "They are working to recruit others. I am confident they will have sufficient forces."

Secretary looked at Syrus inquisitively. "You are confident?" he asked.

"Yes." Syrus said. There was nothing confident about his response. "After we have acquired our recruits, what will be expected of us?"

"You will be expected to keep the Fallen Souls from submitting their requests. More importantly, you will also be expected to get them to revoke any requests already submitted," Secretary respied.

"Revoke?" Sam asked. "Why would anyone want to revoke their original request?" Patho's eyes widened, and his nostrils flared. His appearance was hideous. He was almost unbearable to look at when he had no expression. When he was frustrated or angered, which was most of the time, he became almost impossible to look upon.

"Pit Fear!" Secretary snapped. "They must be so consumed with Pit Fear that any hopes of returning to the Kingdom are extinguished."

"Do you mean torture?" Sam asked with questioning excitement.

"They should be so lucky," Abaddon replied. "Pit Fear is far worse than any torture you could even imagine. Pit Fear is all consuming. It can paralyze the mightiest of men. Pit Fear consumes, controls, and destroys."

"How will we accomplish this?" Sul asked with eyes wide open.

Abaddon watched in rare amusement as all three began twitching in different directions. They are idiots, he thought.

"You will be trained," answered Secretary. "It won't take long. All that is required is a hint of Pit Fear from you, and it will do the rest."

The three were envisioning the horrible acts that must certainly follow Pit Fear. Syrus looked at Secretary with his head slightly tilted, "It?" he asked.

"Yes *IT*," Abaddon snapped. "Pit Fear is alive. The slightest hint of it and IT does the rest. It spreads and multiplies. It devours anything in its path. The only one that can stop it is the King."

Abaddon stopped abruptly. How could he have let that slip? No one mentioned the King in the presence of Patho. He could hear Patho's fiery breaths. They were slow and deep. Abaddon reached his hand out behind Sam just in case his shield services were required. "Pit Fear is Patho's brilliant discovery. Pit Fear is the Pit's number one line of defense."

"It's our only line," Secretary said, very monotone. He cleared his throat, adjusted his posture and continued, "There is no need for any other, Pit Fear is quite adequate. There is yet to be found one who has been able to eliminate it from the mind. Once introduced, it is impossible to get rid of."

"This fear may be real and very effective in Turayn, but you are not speaking of the Humans?" Sul asked. "Is it possible to control them out here in the Darkness?"

"They understand what they have done," Abaddon replied. "They seek forgiveness. Yes, they have the ability to reason, to think, to feel. Let me ask you, what brings you to this table?"

"I guess I never thought about it," Sul answered.

"That's the point. You could think about it," Abaddon said.

"So once we instill Pit Fear, what's next?" Syrus asked. The excitement in all three was growing again. Syrus began bouncing as he sat, his mind filled with thoughts of torture, manipulation, and injury.

"Oh, I want disease!" Sul said in the manner a child would who was listing his birthday gift wishes. "It must be amazing - spreading death and disease around."

"Can I learn Curses?" Sam squinted his eyes as he envisioned the possible effects of casting curses. Without realizing it, he kept nervously raising his hand as if wanting to be recognized. "I could be the cursing-est devil!"

Evil anticipation is so disgusting.

Abaddon and Secretary looked blankly at each other and then back at the three. Syrus eventually realized that they were being stared at. "What are you looking at?" Syrus asked. "We only speak of the actions that most certainly follow?"

"Bahahahaha!" Every head turned toward the door. Serpent was bent over in laughter.

"So good of you to join us," Patho said with a glare. Serpent bowed his head, not as a way of acknowledging Patho, but to miss the object that was soaring toward him. He then un-respectfully saluted Patho.

Serpent continued in his long, drawn out way of pronouncing each word. "An action? There isss never an action! All that isss required is the HHHINT!" Serpent jested in his slow and controlled manner. Sam, Syrus, and Sul were suddenly still. "Do you ever remember a time that a fear actually came true?" Serpent asked.

The three now sat in deep thought. Sam began to jerk. He involuntarily raised his hand before he spoke. "Yes," he offered. "I recall several times saying, 'I knew this was going to happen!'"

"Exxxactly!" said Serpent. "You knew it wasss going to happen. You made it happen! We only instilled the fear." Serpent continued laughing in a deep, evil tone.

"Are you saying that there is never an action planned for each fear?" Syrus asked.

Abaddon rolled his eyes, Secretary flung his head back in annoyance and Patho yelled out, "IDIOT!"

The three sat stupefied, recalling their days in Turayn. Fear had controlled them. Fear had prevented them from so much. Was it possible that there was really nothing to fear? Had their entire time in Turayn been wasted on unsubstantiated fears?

Secretary knew there was danger in allowing them to think too much, or for too long. He quickly moved the meeting forward, "Your training on Pit Fear will begin as soon as this meeting is adjourned, which can't be soon enough. I ask that you choose the strongest of your recruits to also be in attendance." He looked directly at Sul, Syrus, and Sam, ensuring he had their attention. "There will be no further discussion of these so-called fear actions inside or outside the Pit. Our one, and only focus, is to instill Pit Fear. We will let Pit Fear do the rest." He glared at each one, "Is that understood?"

"Yes," the three replied unconfidently in unison.

"We have completed the plans for the holding area," Secretary said.

"Holding area?" sneered Serpent.

"Yes, holding area!" Secretary snapped. "What did you think we were going to do with them – burn them?" Serpent hissed in evil delight.

"We will need an area that confines the Fallen Souls," Secretary continued.

"Our current drawings appear to be sufficient for as long as this mission is active. Chains are being forged which will be held by your recruits. This will be located just behind the Pit."

"If I understand you," Sul said, "there will be a corral created by our recruits linked together by a forged chain?"

"Ah, *shackles for the damned*," Serpent sneered, breaking into a silent, boisterous laugh, as there was no more laughter in him.

"Will this really confine them?" Sam asked.

"It doesn't have to," Abaddon replied, "As long as the Fallen Souls think it will, it will."

"Pit Fear?" Sul asked.

"Exactly. Good to see you've finally shown up," Secretary added, rushing the meeting along. "I believe this is all we have to discuss. Sam, Syrus, and Sul, I'll meet you and your recruits outside."

They had been sitting long enough for the blanket of soot to settle. As they rose, new billows of filth filled the room. The three were still in a state of confusion as they contemplated Pit Fear, causing them to leave without acknowledging anyone in attendance. This didn't seem to bother those who remained.

"Are you aware of what the King isss doing?" Serpent asked directing his attention to Patho, who jerked and snarled. "I sssee you are not." Patho picked up an object from his work table and flung it toward Serpent. Serpent held out his hand and caught it. Abaddon's eyes widened. If he had been the applauding type, he would have. Serpent stared at Patho. Dropping the object to the ground, he continued, "The King has a corral of his own. It is on the opposite side of the Kingdom than Turayn. It appears to be a wall of warriors."

"Warriors?" Abaddon asked. "Why would he need to protect any area outside the Kingdom with warriors?"

"He surrounds Turayn with them," Secretary replied. "A second Turayn?"

"Perhaps he is increasing the Kingdom boundaries with the return of so many from..." Abaddon stopped suddenly; his attention was fixed on Serpent, and he knew it best not to turn his attention to Patho.

"Do you forget who you work for?" Patho screeched.

"NO! Never, your Highest. Just attempting to establish the King's purpose," Abaddon answered, refusing to turn his attention.

"Be careful, or you will find yourself one of the King's purposes," Patho snarled. "Go meet your recruits," Patho ordered.

Abaddon bowed his head, "Yes, your Highest. You have my total allegiance." Abaddon backed out of the room.

As Secretary stood to take his leave, Patho asked, "What of Abaddon's request?"

Secretary looked up at Serpent then to Patho, "Requests are only accepted by the one requesting it."

"What do you mean?" Patho demanded.

"I've tried. I've asked Others to hand it off. The Messengers and Transports know. Don't ask me how, they just do. Abaddon will have to put in the request himself," Secretary said as he crossed his arms.

"Hogwash!" Patho said disgustingly. "He's not ready for that. That will take some doing." Patho paced behind his desk. With each step, new layers of dirt took flight. "Serpent," he ordered, "We need to pressure Abaddon. Between the two of us, we should be able to squeeze him into it."

"Into what?" Serpent asked.

Secretary looked at Patho, "You haven't told him?" he asked. Patho snarled.

"Told me what?" Serpent asked.

Secretary waited for Patho, but there was no response. "Our Highest has plans for Abaddon," Secretary offered. "Plans that apparently now require your assistance."

Secretary stood watching Serpent's reaction. When there wasn't one, he turned and left the room. As he closed the door behind him, he envisioned Abaddon being squeezed between Patho and Serpent. It made him shiver with disgust and delight at the same time.

A moment later, the silence was broken with another outburst.

Serpent had found his laughter.

15

Odella embraced her new responsibility, requiring daily meetings with those who oversaw the requests from the Fallen Souls. Of all the places in the Kingdom that could have been the appointed meeting place, Odella chose the gardens.

Since her return to the Kingdom, the garden had been her refuge. It was there she hid her return. It was the garden where she overheard the Princes' discussion of ending The Plan. This was the place where she found the strength to burst into the Dining Room that afternoon and in doing so, took the first step toward facing her King, Queen, and most importantly, Magnor.

The number of the Fallen Souls requesting their original request for forgiveness be voided had slowed, but not ended. It was discouraging to all. Discouraging - yes, hopeless - no. There was no doubt that the Kingdom's Stronghold would soon protect any Fallen Soul desiring forgiveness.

After this day's meeting, Odella sat quietly under a large olive tree. The breeze gently swayed the delicate branches. In the distance, the groundskeepers were tenderly caring for a patch of deep purple and white flowers. She heard the songs of several birds perched in the trees around her, when she was unexpectedly flooded with memories of her life in Turayn.

They were memories of sitting on a throne. It still seemed impossible that she was Haddad, the ruler of the King's people. How had she ever become a king? She, who was a shepherd boy; she, who was born a boy. How odd Turayn is. Odella thought back to the days as a young boy tending the sheep in the fields. She loved being in the fields of Turayn; perhaps that is why she loved the gardens so. She loved the stillness, the beauty, the freshness in the air. She loved walking with the King.

"May I join you?" The words startled her. She was unaware that anyone had walked up behind her. She didn't have to turn to know who it was.

"Yes, Sire, please join me," she said as she turned toward the King with a glowing smile.

"You were deep in thought, anything you care to share?"

"I have a feeling that You don't need an invitation to join my thoughts. At least you didn't when we – or should I say, I was in Turayn." The King laughed. "You are all knowing, aren't you?" she asked gently.

Now the King had a glowing smile, "Let's keep that our little secret," he replied. "There are but a few with that level of understanding."

"I take that as a great compliment," Odella said, as she moved to one side of the bench.

"It was meant to be one," said the King, as he took a seat next to her.

They sat quietly for a few moments. Odella watched a small bird perched on the bottom branch of a tall, slender tree. It was his coloring that had first drawn her attention. As she observed him, she had felt its contentment, his gentleness. Odella sat motionless, listening to his song. "Why did you spend so much time with me - or Haddad - when I was in Turayn?"

The King had been watching Odella. She had a gentleness, a peace about her that radiated out. How magical it is when beauty observes beauty. "Because you wanted me to. It's that simple. And besides, you were great fun to be with. What a fearless child you were."

"I'm not so sure 'fearless' is the right word. I did a lot of dangerous things." Odella chuckled at the memories as they replayed in her mind. She abruptly stopped, "Why did you let me go after that lion?"

The King put his head back and laughed. "Oh my dear, it was not just the lion, there was also a bear," he reminded her.

Odella's eyes opened wide, then she burst into laughter, "I had forgotten! What were you thinking? I was but a boy!"

"But you were a great boy!" said the King, as he put his hand over his chest, "You had the heart of a king from the very beginning."

Odella shook her head as the scenes replayed over in her mind. While tending his father's sheep, a task he loved, there approached a lion. Without hesitation Haddad grabbed whatever he could put his hands on and went after it. "But why did you let me go after it?"

The King smiled. Odella loved his smile; it was comforting, bringing peace to the center of her being. "You knew that if you did not, he would destroy your flock," the King said. "There had been many times prior when you were faced with a challenge, nothing that compared to the lion or bear, of course. Each time you asked if you should fight; you never went out without asking. By the time the lion and bear came along, you didn't ask, you acted."

"I don't recall you asking my permission, you told me what you wanted to do and asked that I be with you. It was a sign of maturing - and certainly a sign of your strength," said the King. "When it came time to face that foolish giant, you didn't ask or tell. You walked out there and told him what we were going to do. I knew then what kind of king you would become."

She stiffened, tightening her fists as if ready to do it all over again, "He was a beast!"

"That he was. But you took care of him," the King said. "I don't recall you using your fists."

Odella laughed once again. "I did have good intentions, but I messed up so many times."

"That you did," said the King, nodding in agreement.

"Thank goodness you created forgiveness," she said.

"Created?"

"Yes?" Odella said, suddenly second-guessing herself.

"Do you not remember forgiveness before Turayn?" asked the King. "Forgiveness has existed from the beginning."

"But there was no need for it prior to that day!" Odella said boldly.

The King let out a bellow, "My dear, my sweet, sweet child, forgiveness has always been required. Do you think everyone in the Kingdom is perfect?"

"No – well – but they are not like the Humans..."

The King reached out his hand and took Odella's, "Forgiveness has always been a part of our lives. Mistakes are made, errors happen. Prior to Patho's upheaval, forgiveness was requested and given freely."

The King watched Odella as she contemplated his words. He too was filled with memories of her life in Turayn. Was it any wonder Haddad had been one of his favorites? He loved her as a boy. He marveled at her strength and determination as she grew. She won his heart all over again when she became king.

Then as quickly as a blink, she turned to him and asked, "How is it that you don't know?"

"Don't know what?" he asked inquisitively.

"How is it that you are unaware of who the Fallen Souls are? You know all..." Odella said rather boldly.

The King put his head back and bellowed once again, "You are one of a kind, my dear!" He put his arm on the back of the bench and Odella felt safe. "I have chosen to allow Free Will to be a part of the Kingdom and Turayn. In doing so, I have allowed there to be a few ... boundaries. Free Will is what allowed you and the others to leave, in doing so there was a separation that happened between us."

"Like the separation felt between you and Jael?" Odella asked.

"Not quite. The Fallen Soul's separation was allowed because of Free Will - but driven by evil intent. Jael had no evil intent. It was his Free Will that allowed him to become the great sacrifice, that was driven only by love."

Odella began to well up; a tear escaped her control. She had thought she understood Jael's purpose in Turayn, but as the King spoke, there was a new depth to her understanding.

"The separation was necessary so Jael could once and forever overcome the control evil intent has on any soul. He created an even playing field for all. Free Will remains, but evil intent can no longer control." The King paused. "That didn't really answer your question though, did it?"

"Why do I not know who the Fallen Souls are? There are two reasons: the first is I choose not to, and the second is that there is a separation of our souls. I was no longer connected to the Fallen Souls as I was when they were in the Kingdom. That was until Jael's sacrifice. Now, we have been reconnected." The King stopped as a gardener passed by.

"You mean you can reconnect once the Human seeks forgiveness – right?" Odella asked.

The King hesitated. "We are connected."

"All of them? Even those who reject Jael's teachings."

"Jael's sacrifice was for all. They may not know it or accept it, but what Jael did, he did for every Fallen Soul that has and will enter Turayn. He reconnected all." The King paused. "Unforgiveness is extremely powerful. Unforgiveness does not exist in the Kingdom."

"Why not?"

The King thought for a moment. "Let me put it in the words of a wise human king who once ruled in Turayn - If You, oh King, kept records on wrongdoings, who would stand a chance?"

Without hesitation, Odella joined in,
As it turns out, forgiveness is Your habit, and that's why You are worshiped, feared, and honored.

"I wrote that, didn't I?" she asked with childish pride.

"It's a wonderful thought," replied the King.

"Forgiveness is yours!" Odella said.

"Correct," said the King.

"By not offering forgiveness, I am placing myself above you?" she asked.

"By choosing not to forgive, one is saying that they hold the authority to judge. When un-forgiveness is witnessed in the Kingdom, it is quickly identified and just as quickly dealt with."

"Why is it not so obvious in Turayn?" Odella asked.

"In Turayn, one is able to mask their unforgiveness. Pride, envy, abuse, neglect, birthright; a Human can cover their unforgiveness so deeply that it takes a lifetime to find. But it is there! It is always there."

"Does seeking forgiveness uncover unforgiveness?" Odella asked.

"For some it does," answered the King. "There are those who, once they seek forgiveness, realize that they must forgive. It would be considered a selfish child who received a gift but was unwilling to share it. For others, it will take them their entire life to understand. The act of forgiveness is what stands between enjoying a life in Turayn or struggling through every day."

The King reached over and touched Odella's arm, "Haddad understood forgiveness. Haddad knew where forgiveness came from; he understood that without it his life would be nothing. He also understood that he must offer it as well. The Human life is nothing until the eyes of their souls are opened to the act of forgiveness."

Odella repeated the words softly, "If You, oh King, kept records on wrongdoings, who would stand a chance? As it turns out, forgiveness is Your habit, and that's why You are worshiped, feared, and honored." Odella sighed, "It's not only Your habit, forgiveness belongs to You."

"Yes, dear, it does belong to me, but I freely offer it. It is my desire that all will receive it."
Odella stood and walked slowly around the bench. The garden was suddenly quiet with no one in sight. Odella leaned over the back of the bench and asked unexpectedly, "What of Palti?"

The King looked back at her. "What brought you to Palti?"

She swung around the corner of the bench and took her seat once again. "Do you truly not know where he is?" she asked with a suspenseful look.

He looked away and sighed deeply. Odella sat patiently. Her inquisitiveness was quickly turning to regret. She suddenly felt the weight of her question. With each second, she wished she could take back her words.

The King returned his attention to her, "No. I do not."

"But you could, right?" she asked.

"Yes, I could. I could send a million warriors out to find him and bring him home," the King answered.

"But, you won't," she said staring into his eyes.

"No. No, I will not." he said. "If I were to bring him home apart from his choosing, nothing would be gained. It is up to him to choose." Odella could see the pain in the King's expression. She reached out and took his hand.

"I am sorry," she said as her eyes welled up. "I am sorry that you have had to suffer the loss because of our ... our selfishness." She squeezed the King's hand. Placing her other hand over his, she gently soothed it. Compared to his hands, Odella's looked miniature. A tear landed on the back of her hand.

Without looking up, she quietly asked, "Why was it said that Haddad had a heart after the King? I made so many, many foolish mistakes. They were not always innocent; there were many times they were driven by evil intent."

"Do you recall what you did after each of these so-called events?"

Odella paused and wiped a remaining tear from her cheek. "I sought your forgiveness."

"That is what made you great," said the King. "You understood your humanness, you saw its faults and you understood my forgiveness and power. Even before Jael's time, you believed."

"Is it really that simple?" she asked.

"It is that simple. It is that difficult." The King put his hand over Odella's and patted it gently. Odella smiled. "Speaking of battles, tell me the latest of the requests." The King sat patiently as Odella updated him on the most recent reports of the Fallen Souls.

Odella had walked daily with the King during her time in Turayn; now she was seated next to him. It was a gift she would never again take for granted.

16

As Tayten approached the Dining Room, he could hear the discussion. Turning to the steward accompanying him, he said, "they are still in there. Inform the kitchen that this meeting will run right up until dinner. We will need to prepare and set for dinner with as little disturbance as possible." Tayten opened the doors to the Dining Room as the steward returned to the kitchen.

Tayten's entrance wasn't noticed, as the six sitting around the table were deep in discussion.

"I believe one hundred men is sufficient," Waldemar had the floor. "We don't want this to look like an attack. It's going to draw enough attention as it is. We also do not want to run the risk of not having enough to provide adequate protection."

"Yes, that is our greatest concern," said the King. "Ferrul, go back to the beginning and lay this out for us again."

Ferrul stood as he began, "Magnor will select his regiment of one hundred warriors. There will be seven days of training before leaving for the Stronghold. Once there, they will spend a short time as extra support for the outer wall."

"And why is that important?" Waldemar asked.

"It allows them time in the Darkness while being protected. More importantly, it gives them their first glimpse of the Fallen Souls who have already found their way into the safety of the Stronghold," Carasi said. "It is assumed that most of those accompanying Magnor have experience outside the Kingdom, but guarding Turayn is much different than surrounding the Stronghold."

"No one is sure what we are going to find out there," Magnor said.

Ferrul looked around the table to ensure all questions had been asked and sufficiently answered.

"Magnor will then take his select and begin their journey. They will proceed through the darkness to the Pit. We expect that whatever Patho is doing, he is doing it on the far side of the Pit."

"Father, have you heard who were the first to volunteer for this mission?" Magnor asked. "The five you assigned to transport the Pit."

Smiling with delight, the King said, "They may be the only troop you need."

"Magnor will make a wide circle around the Pit. If there is nothing to see," Ferrul looked directly at Magnor, "you must return quickly. There cannot be any last-minute changes. No one decides to go farther out, not on this mission." Ferrul waited for Magnor's acknowledgment. He continued, "Upon returning to the Stronghold, the men will be under close observation for the first two days. They will select a friend or family member who they desire to be at the camp waiting for their return. We are not taking any chances."

"Magnor, have you begun your selection?" the King asked.

"Father," it was the first time Quaine had spoken up all afternoon. "I would like to join Magnor in this mission. I would also like to offer ten of the Redeemed Warriors to join us."

"Do you think that is wise?" asked the King.

"Are you sure you want to do that?" asked Waldemar.

"I am Father. And I believe there are ten warriors that I have been training who are also ready and very capable of this assignment."

"I'm sorry, Quaine," Carasi said, "but you must know that this brings many concerns. It was but a short time ago that we were concerned you were making plans to leave."

"Those were not just concerns," Waldemar said, addressing Carasi, "they were real."

"Yes, they were real," Quaine admitted. "But they are no longer. None of us will ever completely put to rest the struggles in returning to the Kingdom. It is now a part of who we are. I see that. I know it firsthand. I have also seen firsthand the strength and determination that comes with fighting such a battle. Those warriors who Waldemar and I are training have a strength and integrity that matches, and in most cases, supersedes the others. They are not only fighting to protect the Kingdom, they are fighting from within."

"Are you sure you are ready to face the darkness?" Magnor asked.

"I have given it a great deal of thought. I will admit there is hesitation. The last time I was out there, I was one of them. Have I wondered if somehow Patho would see me and find a way to hold me? Yes, I have. Have I questioned that I would be unable to face the reality of the Fallen Souls, and be somehow forced to stay out there with them? Yes. Have I wondered if the effects of the darkness could be stronger and more damaging to someone who has already spent time there? Of course, I've thought of it all."

"Do you really believe there are ten within the ranks of the Redeemed Warriors who would be willing to go?" asked Ferrul.

Quaine was filled with emotional confidence. Taking a deep breath, he said, "They are all willing to go. Every one of them has approached me with their request." The room was silent.

"Perhaps Waldemar and Quaine are training a group of warriors who will exceed everyone's expectations. Perhaps these will be the ones..." the King paused. "I have no concerns."

Each at the table looked at the others for confirmation. Breaking the silence, Magnor pushed his chair back, leaned over the table, and extended his hand to Quaine. "I would be honored for you to join me. And for those ten that you have chosen, we must get them integrated with the others as quickly as possible."

Quaine cringed with excitement. "We will be honored to be included," he said, accepting Magnor's hand.

The Dining Room doors opened a moment later. The group was expecting Tayten to be standing there surrounded by attendants and stewards. To their delight, the Queen and Odella entered the room.

"We understand there is some intense planning going on in here," said the Queen. "Thought you may need our assistance." The men laughed as they welcomed the two in.

"We do need your assistance," Carasi said. "We are finishing the details for Magnor's inspection of Patho's..." Carasi stopped, "I have no idea what to call it."

"None of us will until we see it," Quaine said.

"We?" asked Odella, looking at Quaine and then at Magnor.

"Yes, we," Magnor said. "Quaine has volunteered to join me." Odella's expression immediately changed. "Don't tell me you are concerned for his safety now."

Odella looked at the Queen for reassurance. As desired, the Queen's eyes were full of confidence and her smile was comforting.

"You will be there when I return, won't you? You are my selected 'friend'," Magnor said reaching out for her hand.

"And, Mother," Quaine said, "I would like for you to be there as well."

"It will be my honor," said the Queen.

"What about me?" asked the King jokingly.

"It will never matter how old or important they become, they will always be my boys," the Queen said, as she bent over and kissed the King on the cheek. "You can be here, waiting for me." They didn't witness it often, but there were times that the Queen drew out a boyish grin from the King. This would be one to remember.

"Awww," said Konnory. "Someday I'll have my very own Queen. Well, actually she will be a princess, since I am not a King. But then some day she and I will be King and Queen and then I will have my very own Queen..."

Jael sat across from Konnory, resting his chin on his fists. He began to look at those sitting around the table. Each had turned their attention toward Konnory, as he continued his deliberation on Kings, Queens, Princesses, and Princes. A few glanced at Jael and back to Konnory. "...if we have sons, they will be Princes themselves..."

Jael spoke up over Konnory's chant, "He's been hanging around Balbas too long. If we don't stop him, he'll find a way to make this go on till dinner is served."

"How do you stop him?" asked the King.

"I usually give him a treat," Jael answered, very matter of factly.

As the group burst into laughter, the doors opened, and to everyone's delight it was Tayten and his troop. Within minutes the table was prepared, candles lit, and a feast perfectly arranged on the serving tables.

17

The day had finally arrived for the inspection of the Pit. The King and Queen, along with Odella and Waldemar, waited outside the castle doors for their fearless warriors. Magnor exited first. He was in full uniform - every button, snap, and tie was in place. Odella's heart began to race as his steps brought him closer. He saluted his Father, gave the Queen a gentle kiss, and embraced Odella. Odella's heart raced faster.

"It will be all right," he whispered. "You'll be there when I return."

Quaine was next to appear. He, too, was in full uniform. Something none of them had witnessed since he had left the Kingdom. The King saluted, the Queen embraced, Waldemar teared up, and Odella bowed. There was a boldness that they had not seen before. As he turned and followed Magnor, the King whispered to the Queen, "He will be a force to be reckoned with." She simply nodded in agreement.

Magnor and Quaine followed the instructions explicitly. The troop's first stop was at the Stronghold. It was empowering to stand among the outer wall and feel the strength and protection that seemed to flow out from their beings. There was great contrast between the strength of the warriors and the Fallen Souls they were there to protect. What was immediately apparent to Quaine was the absence of interaction between the two groups. He understood why such a divide was necessary. He could only imagine how difficult it was for either side.

The morning of the mission arrived. Magnor, Quaine, ninety warriors, and ten redeemed boarded their chariots. "Men, you understand our mission. There is to be no deterrence from it. Once we have returned, we will have time to discuss what we are about to witness. Until then, stay focused. Stay aware." With those words, Magnor grabbed the reigns and they were off.

It was a far cry from the army that accompanied Magnor the day he brought Jael home from the Pit. This was not a battle. This was not to be an attack. This was a mission to inspect what they believed Patho had established in order to stop the Fallen Souls from making their requests for forgiveness.

In the lead were the five warriors the King had assigned to move the Pit out into the Darkness, now many years ago. They didn't need instructions. None of them would ever forget that assignment or where the Pit was placed.

Upon their approach to the Pit, the five veered far to the outside in hopes of avoiding too much attention. From the rear of the Pit, they began to hear horrific noises: moaning and muffled cries. As the sounds grew louder, they could see in the distance a massive cluster of beings. Within moments, they witnessed first hand Patho's very own stronghold.

Its walls were made up of what appeared to be fallen souls holding chains. There was no structure, no reason for any of those confined to feel they were unable to break free. The cries grew louder.

As they passed, the Fallen Souls held within the boundaries began reaching out as if they were asking to be freed. Their anguish grew louder. The moaning at times bordered on screams. The site was far worse than anyone, including Magnor, had anticipated.

Magnor immediately looked at his brother and shouted, "Go to your men!"

"They will be all right," Quaine responded.

"Will you?" Magnor asked.

"Yes." Quaine answered with great strength. "Will you?"

As the regiment continued on, passing those being held captive, each felt moments of being sucked down. Each fought the pull. But each entertained the thought of breaking away and swooping down to break the chains. Each resisted, but it took all their strength.

The anticipation and excitement that was felt at the beginning of the mission had left when they saw Patho's confines for what they were. Silence and heaviness filled the air on the journey back. As they approached the King's Stronghold, Magnor made a sudden change.

"We will not stop," he ordered. "Proceed to the Kingdom!" Quaine did not hesitate or question.

Their return surprised those waiting at the camp. The warriors remained in their chariots, waiting for there to be a final count. When all were accounted for, Magnor turned and addressed the group, "What we witnessed today was at the very least unexpected. There is nothing that compares in past or present. It would have been unwise to have stayed with those guarding the Stronghold."

Magnor looked at Quaine. The brothers locked on each other. What they had observed behind the Pit was overwhelming. The Fallen Souls crying out for help, in unbearable anguish, bound and confined within a weak fortress; nothing visibly holding them. Why would they allow themselves to be held in such a way? What could possibly have been said to them to make them believe they had no way of escape? What was this hold Patho had? Magnor was beginning to realize what Quaine had been through; he was beginning to see, even if he could not understand, life in the Darkness.

Unable to speak any further, Quaine continued Magnor's address, "Until further notice, you will not leave. We ask that any conversation containing details of what we observed be protected to this group only. While we remain confined together, you are free, and encouraged, to discuss any and all events of this day. We will not adjourn or invite anyone to join us until all, that means every one of us, has had time to discuss and process this day's events. Magnor and I will be available at all times." Quaine looked at Magnor. Magnor nodded in agreement.

Quaine continued, "Provisions are being prepared, but we have caught them off guard with our early return." Quaine smiled a reassuring smile. "A job well done! I am proud to be among you."

If this had been any other mission, there would have been a loud round of cheers and celebration. But not today. Today there was silence. Today there was a reverence. Today there was a new understanding of life outside the Gates.

A messenger was sent to the castle to inform the King of Magnor's early arrival. Waldemar happened to be returning to the castle at the same time. The two met at the front door.

"What brings you here?" Waldemar asked in a tone of concern.

"I was sent to inform the King of...," the warrior said, "...I was sent to see the King." Without hesitation, Waldemar escorted the warrior to the Throne Room. There they found both the King and Queen.

"Sire, you have a messenger," Waldemar said rather abruptly.

"Come in," the King instructed. The warrior drew closer, saluted both King and Queen, and stood at attention. "What word do you have for us?"

"Sire, I was sent to inform you that Magnor and Quaine have returned to the Kingdom earlier than expected. They, and the warriors who accompanied them, are settling into the camp."

"Were you prepared for them?" the King asked.

"Not this early, but I am sure that by now all is in order," replied the messenger.

"I will be there shortly," said the King. He put his hand on the arms of the throne in preparation for taking his leave. The Queen reached out and placed her hand on his.

"I will go," she said.

The King looked at her. "Are you sure?" he asked.

"Yes." It was all the confirmation he needed. Addressing Waldemar, she instructed, "Prepare my things." She stood, and leaned over to kiss the King. "I'll send word," she said, and made her way to the door.

Odella had seen the warrior and Waldemar entering the castle from the gardens. She was coming around the corner, almost running into the Queen. "What is it? What is wrong?" she asked.

"They have returned early. They are safe, they are within the Kingdom," the Queen replied.

"I will go with you," Odella said.

The Queen reached out, placed her hands on Odella's shoulders, requiring her full attention. "You will collect the friends and family members who were chosen to make the journey and inform them they need to leave today. Each should select two additional relations to accompany them." The Queen paused, looking Odella in the eyes. "There is no room for fear here. We will not act in response to fear." A tear began to escape the corner of Odella's eye. "They are safe within the Kingdom. Now go, you have a task to accomplish." The Queen released Odella, "I will see you at the camp."

"Waldemar, we need to get word that there will be two to three hundred more joining us. You know what supplies will be needed. Make arrangements for the rest to be sent. We should not only plan for the additional people, but also additional days."

"Yes," Waldemar said, bowing his head, as he turned and headed down the hall.

The Queen addressed to the messenger, "I trust you know the way back?" With boldness the messenger nodded. "Then lead on. I will be by your side."

As the King watched the two walk out of sight he softly repeated, "I will be by your side. A gentle smile replaced the concerned look of moments ago. "Son, you have no idea how amazing it is to have her by your side."

The Queen and warrior boarded the chariot and were off, leaving the Queen's attendants to prepare her previsions for the trip. As they entered the camp, servants rushed over to greet the Queen. "It's an honor to have you here."

"Thank you. Where are my sons?" she asked.

"I'll take you to them," the messenger offered. The two walked toward a large tent. The Queen could hear their voices from a distance. She made her way to the opening and stood quietly. Magnor was the first to notice. He jumped to his feet and ran to her. As they embraced, each held the other tightly. Magnor could feel her warm love through the embrace.

"It's so good to see you," he said softly. They stood for what seemed an eternity. Mother looked over at Quaine, who stood motionless watching the reunion. She put her hand out and signaled for him to join them. He didn't need any more coaxing than that. Rushing toward her, she opened her arms wider and cradled both. The boys felt warm, safe, and whole. They began to breath slowly and deeply, as if they were taking her in.

As they began to pull themselves away, the Queen softly said, "You have returned sooner than expected." Both nodded. "Tell me what happened."

"It's horrifying," Magnor began. "I'm not sure I can put it into words."

The Queen looked at Quaine, "And you?" she asked.

"I was expecting the worst, but there was something... something indefinable in what we saw," Quaine replied. The three walked over to a small table and sat. The Queen held out her hands and took the hand of each boy.

"Tell me about it," she said. Magnor hesitated.

"Mother, they are in such torment, such sounds of anguish I have never experienced," Quaine said. "As I heard the screams from the distance, I was expecting to see them bound with chains or confined within prison walls."

"They were not?" the Queen asked.

"No," replied Magnor.

"No, not at all. Patho has created his own stronghold. It is simply Fallen Souls holding what appeared to be chains."

"What keeps them there?" Magnor asked.

"Fear," replied the Queen. Both looked at her. She squeezed their hands. Of course, that was Patho's power over them, fear.

"They could escape at any time, but they don't see it," Magnor said.

"What else could Patho possibly do to them? Separating them from Father is the supreme act. He has them in bondage and torment based on fear." Quaine's words were a statement and question at the same time.

"How are the other warriors?" the Queen asked.

"They are bothered, deeply affected," Magnor answered. "Mother, there were moments that we all felt we were being drawn into their fear. I knew that if I allowed it for a single moment to take hold, I would be sucked into the midst of those tortured Souls."

"Don't think for a moment you wouldn't have been," Mother replied. "Patho's fear is powerful."

"Quaine's team seems to be handling it better than the rest," Magnor offered.

"That they would," the Queen said. "They have a better understanding of the Darkness. I would like to see them."

"Are you sure?" Magnor asked.

"Of course, she is sure," Quaine said. "They are together this afternoon. We have asked that they remain reserved when any of the attendants are present. But we are giving them time when they don't have to be guarded, time they are free to speak of the experience openly."

"How wise you both are," she said. "Take me to them."

Quaine took hold of the Queen's arm. Magnor made his way to the other side and held out his arm. Mother took it as well. As they walked, both boys could feel her love and strength permeating their souls.

The warriors had been taken to a small meadow surrounded by rows of tall, stately trees; the trees created a barrier to the outside world. It felt safe, it felt comfortable, and most of all, it felt protected.

As the three walked through the trees, the Queen could see the warriors spread out around the meadow - some standing, some pacing. Others were sitting in a small group. A few were lying on their backs looking up into the sky. As they drew closer, the Queen could hear soft rumblings. There were multiple of conversations going on all at once. The moment one of the warriors noticed them approaching, a hush began to fall across the group. The Queen entered the center of the group and said, "No need to stop on my account. I want to hear everything you have to say." There was reluctance by all of them.

"It's all right," Quaine instructed. He pointed to one of his redeemed warriors. "Tell the Queen what you saw," he said. Taking Quaine's lead, the Queen turned her attention directly to the warrior. As she drew close to him, his peripheral vision blurred. When she was standing face to face with him, all the world around him disappeared. For that moment, it was only the Queen and a warrior.

He began to speak of what he saw. The Queen listened intently to each of their stories. She didn't rush anyone. She cried when they cried. She held them when they were too weak to support themselves. Hours passed, as the Queen received each of her warriors.

Odella had done what was instructed of her. She arrived with three hundred friends and family members who had one purpose: To make themselves available when the warriors needed them. The group was quiet and restrained. Many were anxious. A meal had been prepared, but few were able to partake. Gathered in small clusters, unsure of what was expected of them, Odella called over one of the commanders. "Where are they?" she asked.

"The Queen has been with them most of the day. They are all camped in a small field just past those trees."

Odella stood looking toward the area. It took all her strength not to run in that direction. Her thoughts were interrupted by a hand on her shoulder. It was the wife of one of the five warriors who led the charge. "What are we to do?" she asked.

Odella shook her head. "I'm not sure." The woman reached down and took Odella's hand. The two stood motionless. Odella began to hum. It was a simple tune. It was a song all children learned in the Kingdom. It spoke of the King's love and protection of his children. The second time through, she was joined by her new companion. One by one, each of those who had made this journey of uncertainty joined in. Hand in hand, softly singing a child's lullaby. As the circle grew, they walked slowly toward the trees that separated them from their loved ones. "He loves us so..." softly filled the air. They repeated the song over and over.

As the last of the warriors finished his conversation with the Queen, they began to hear the soft gentle voices. "He loves us so..."

"Go to her," she said, looking at Magnor. Magnor stood unsure for only a moment. He then turned and ran toward the music. Creating his own path through the trees, he stopped abruptly.

There standing before him was a line of brothers and sisters from the Kingdom. They stood hand in hand. It was so different from what he had witnessed in the darkness. These stood connected by love for their family members and their King.

It only took moments for the other warriors to follow. They too stopped as soon as they saw the chorus. Without instruction, the warriors formed an inner circle, standing shoulder to shoulder. Each felt the strength that flowed through their connection. They felt the protection that flowed from those creating the outer circle.

"He loves us so..." the warriors began to join in.

The Queen and Quaine remained, now being the only ones in the middle of the field. They were hand in hand, listening to the beautiful sound.

"They have no idea, Mother," Quaine said. "They have no idea that there is nothing to fear."

"I know my son," she said. "They will soon realize it as well." Quaine squeezed her hand tightly.

"He loves us so..." filled the air. Those words filled each who were present. It filled their souls and removed their fears.

18

Odella and the Queen remained at the camp for several days. Each warrior was closely watched and evaluated. No one would be allowed to return until they had fully dealt with their experience in the Darkness. Carasi and Ferrul had left for the camp, feeling the need to see and hear firsthand of Patho's confines.

The day of their return, the Queen and Odella were greeted by the King, Konnory, and Jael. As the chariots arrived, the three walked out anxiously to meet them. With warm embraces, the Queen and Odella were welcomed home.

"How were they when you left?" Jael asked.

"Healing," the Queen replied. "There are only a handful who continue to struggle, but I believe it won't take long. I suspect that through their struggling, there will arise a deeper insight of how to address Patho's plan."

"And you, my dear," the King said addressing Odella, "How are you?"

"I am well," answered Odella confidently. "It wasn't easy, but it was good to be among so many friends. Magnor is doing well. And Quaine, all are amazed. There is a strength in him that none of us have ever seen."

"Yes, there is no deficiency in him. For that matter, none of the Redeemed Warriors are showing any signs, it is just the opposite. They all show signs of continued strength," said the Queen.

"The Redeemed Warriors will continue to strengthen, not only within themselves, but also in their numbers. They will become a vital part of the Kingdom's army," said the King.

"Father has arranged dinner in the gardens tonight. It's in celebration of your return." Konnory said.

"How lovely," the Queen said. "Dinner in the garden is perhaps one of my favorite things."

"Dinner with you is one of my favorite things," the King offered. "I believe there are few surprises planned for tonight."

"Really?" asked Jael "I don't think I've been made aware."

"Oh, you will," Konnory offered. "You'll be made very aware." Those who had accompanied the Queen and Odella gathered their belongings and escorted them back to the Castle.

"Jael, isn't it time for the Freedom Celebration in Turayn?" asked the King.

"Yes, they should be preparing for it now."

"If I recall, you loved that time of year," said the King.

"Yes, I did. I had hoped to bring it back to the Kingdom, but it just doesn't seem the same," said Jael.

"Well, tonight we will talk in length of the Freedom Celebration," said the King.

Jael nodded. "I will look forward to that." With another nod, he turned and walked away.

Konnory followed him but was stopped when he felt the King's hand on his shoulder, "He'll be very pleased tonight," He said softly. Konnory nodded in agreement.

⚬⚬

Shortly after Magnor and Quaine had left on their mission, Konnory had what he thought was a brilliant idea. While Jael was occupied elsewhere, Konnory bolted down the center stairwell in hopes of finding Balbas.

As hoped, Balbas was just finishing up with a group of Watchers. He glanced over and spotting Konnory, finished up quickly, and motioned for Konnory to join him.

"I need your help," he began. Balbas smiled with anticipation.

"Are we going after the young ruler? It's about time! Do you have your speech ready? I've been waiting for this!" Balbas said, rubbing his hands together in excitement.

"No, it's not that. Sorry, you'll have to wait a while longer." Balbas' excitement turned rapidly to disappointment. "I need the file on Yerde."

"Yerde? He's been back in the Kingdom almost as long as you."

"I know. When Jael was in Turayn he loved the Freedom Celebration."

"The one Yerde began?"

"The very one. With Father's assistance, we are going to recreate it here in the Kingdom."

Balbas put both hands over his mouth. His eyes glistened with joy. "What a beautiful gesture," he said. "The Freedom Celebration here."

"So, I need Yerde's file," Konnory said.

"Of course, you do. Are you planning on asking Yerde to join you?"

"I am now!" Konnory replied.

"Oh, it will be special."

"You'll be able to witness it first hand,"

"Me? Me, Sir? I'd be included in the evening's festivities in the gardens?"

"But, of course."

"But I never leave this place."

"It's time to get out, the fresh air will do you good," Konnory said. "Now, help me find his file."

The two ascended to the file room and located the shelf containing Yerde's file.

"Will you be taking it to the gardens to read?" the attendant asked.

"Not this time," Konnory replied. "I think I'll sit at my table." With file in hand, Konnory walked to the table that was always prepared for him and took a seat. Looking down at the single file, he rubbed his finger over the name, Yerde. As he opened it, the words on the pages came to life.

> Many years had passed since Nadav's reign in
> Egypt. Nadav had brought his father and brothers
> to this foreign land and it became home to them.
> Their numbers greatly multiplied, and with each
> generation they became an established presence in
> the land.

The ruler who showed such confidence and trust in
Nadav had long passed. With the passing of each of
his successors, Nadav's descendants found less and
less favor.

Around the time Yerde was born, the current
ruler became excessively fearful of the strength
and influence of Nadav's people. In an attempt
to control their numbers, he ordered all male
descendants be put to death.

Yerde's mother was a wise and gentle woman.
Making every attempt to protect the newest member
of her family, she made a cradle out of a basket.

She lined it with pitch, making it waterproof. Each
morning, she took her son and his older sister to the
river bed, where she placed the infant in the basket
and set it in the tall grass along the shore. She left
the girl to watch over the young child and returned
to her duties. At the end of her day, she would
joyfully retrieve the two and hide them safely in
her care until the next day. Each day walking to the
river, once to hide and once to find.

"We just can't get away from using boats to save people, can
we?" Konnory asked, recalling the day the King closed the
door of Latzof's big boat. "If it worked for all creation, I guess
it could work for a baby." Konnory continued reading.

Midway through her day, she was surprised by the

call of her daughter. Hand in hand, they returned
to the river to find the Princess of the land cradling
the boy in her arms. They watched through the
tall grass as the Princess gently rocked him and
sang sweet lullabies. Mother watched as a stranger
comforted her precious belonging. Without
realizing it, her daughter had left her side and was
quickly approaching the gathering.

"You'll need someone to care for him, I know a
woman who has a boy just his age and would be a
very good nurse for you." The girl stood confidently,
reaching her hand up to touch the child's face.

"And where did you come from?" the Princess
asked.

"I was just walking along the shore over there,"
she answered. "Would you like for me to fetch the
woman?" Mother was amazed by her confidence
and clarity of mind.

"Yes, that would be helpful," the Princess replied.
"We'll wait here for you."

The girl ran toward her mother, and in short time
both walked out of the tall grasses and into the
presence of the Princess and the boy.

"Mother makes it look like she has nothing to do in Turayn, but this proves differently. I'd bet Turayn that this was her plan." Konnory continued reading.

> Yerde grew up in the castle under the care of his own mother. He was treated as royalty and trained as a warrior. At the same time, his own people were being treated more and more like slaves.
>
> One day as he walked through a large construction sight, Yerde witnesses the beating of one of his people. He stepped into to protect the man and in doing so, killed his attacker. As Yerde stood over the lifeless body, fear overtook him. Without a second thought, he fled into the great wilderness. There, he found a small village of people where he settled in and tried to forget his former life.
>
> After many years living in the wilderness, the King declared it was time to get his attention. Yerde was tending to one of his flocks when he noticed smoke coming from behind a large boulder. Yerde approached cautiously. Behind the boulder he found a large bush engulfed in flames. As he watched the flames grow, he realized that the fire was not spreading, nor did it seem to be consuming the bush. The King had his attention.
>
> The King instructed Yerde that he would be the one to free his people from the oppression they lived under. He was less than willing. Yerde pulled out

all the excuses he could find, but the King never
ran out of patience or answers. Finally, after great
coaxing, Yerde returned in hopes of freeing his
people.

The King instructed Yerde to address the ruler and
ask for the release of his people. Yerde did so, and
with the help of a few tricks from the King, was quite
impressive with his requests.

Konnory thumbed through the pages. "Plagues? Frogs, locus,
boils, darkness - where does He come up with this stuff?
Konnory jump a few pages further. "The Angel of Death!
What? Father, what were you thinking? I guarantee Magnor
was in on this one. It sounds just like him." He read on.

Yerde promised the ruler of the land that death
would hit the first born on every household. The
King made a way of escape for his people. They
were to kill a lamb and place the blood over their
doorway as a sign to the Angel of Death to pass over
their house.

That night, many innocent infants took their final
breath. For those who had obeyed the Kings
instruction, life was sustained. The Freedom
Celebration was created that night. A time of
remembering the protection of the true King.

Konnory closed the file. "This is it. This is what we are going
to celebrate."

19

As evening arrived, the garden was glowing in celebration. Tables set with the finest linens, gold and silver serving pieces, and candles illuminated the entire garden. Konnory and Jael were among the last to arrive.

Jael was surprised with the number of people in attendance. "I thought Father said this was going to be a small dinner celebrating Mother and Odella's return?" he asked as they made their way in.

"There were a few last minute changes," Konnory replied. He led Jael to the head table.

"This is an unusual table setting."

"This isn't a usual dinner," Konnory offered with a grin.

"An intimate dinner?" Jael asked, looking around the gardens.

"We are celebrating more than their homecoming," Konnory said, as he motioned for an attendant to approach. Konnory directed Jael to the middle of the head table. They stood looking out over the other tables. As the attendant drew closer, Jael could see that he had a cloth carefully draped across his arms. Jael recognized it immediately.

"A prayer cloth? Why does he have a...?" Jael asked.

"Tonight my brother, we have brought the Freedom Celebration to the Kingdom," Konnory answered with great delight.

"Is this your doing? I had so hoped to be able to partake this year, but I never dreamed it would be here, with you, and Father."

"We will all be celebrating it tonight," said the King walking up behind Jael. "But it doesn't look as if we can begin just yet. We are waiting for our guest of honor."

Jael looked over the King's shoulder and saw the Queen and Odella in the distance. "I believe they have arrived," he said.

"There are still a few others arriving," Konnory assured. The attendant stood patiently to the side, across his outstretched arms was Jael's prayer cloth. "This one is for you," Konnory said, as he took the cloth and draped it over Jael's shoulders. Jael had worn such a cloth when he was in Turayn. Memories of teaching in the Temple flooded his mind.

"Will you be wearing the other one?" Jael asked. "Or is it for Father?" Jael felt the cloth with his hands. "This didn't come from Turayn," he said with delight. "This is from the Kingdom."

"Yes, Konnory had them made here," said the King.

"So who else is joining us?" Jael asked with great excitement.

"You'll see, be patient." Konnory scanned the garden in anticipation of his honored guest. "There he is, I see him now," Konnory walked past Jael and toward a small group entering the garden. He greeted each one and then turned and led them to Jael. "Jael, I would like for you to meet Yerde." Jael was expressionless. "I see he is speechless, doesn't happen often."

Jael stretched out his hand in greeting. "I know who you are or were. It's a great honor for you to join us."

"Words cannot possibly express my feelings in meeting you," Yerde reached out his hand in greeting. "It is an honor for my family and I to join you in this celebration. To be able to celebrate it with you. It is beyond my words."

"This is truly a surprise. A great surprise," Jael said as he turned to Konnory. "What made you think of seeking Yerde out?"

"Who better to have at our first celebration than the one who led the first celebration in Turayn," Konnory answered, placing his hand on Jael's shoulder. "Actually, it was Balbas's idea."

"Is Balbas joining us?"

"He is," Konnory said, looking around. "But I'm sure he'll be late. He's a little passionate about rescuing his Humans. I know he'll be here in time for us to start."

Konnory took the second cloth and draped it over Yerde's shoulders. Tears welled up in his eyes as his hand gently felt the fabric and continued down to the tassel that flowed from the edges.

"When I first contacted Yerde, he informed me that he and his family have kept the celebration each year."

"And with each year, more and more join us," Yerde said. "In Turayn, this celebration had great meaning. Now, after returning to the Kingdom, its original meaning pales in comparison. The Freedom Celebration is no longer about being held captive in Turayn; it's about being set free in the Kingdom."

Konnory motioned for Jael to take his seat. He led Yerde to his place of honor. From a distance, he heard the commotion as Balbas entered the garden. In his usual fashion, he was so overwhelmed by it's beauty and significance of the evening that he had become over-excited and felt faint. He was quickly revived and escorted to his seat.

Yerde stood, as all in attendance began to sit. He acknowledged Jael with a nod, and then looked at the King. It took him a moment to regain his composure. "You see," he began, "in

Turayn I was unable to speak clearly; I used it as an excuse for not being able to do as the King had requested." Yerde smiled and shook his head. "But, as we all know him to be, his patience outlasted my excuses."

Yerde looked across the guests seated in front of him. The light of the luminaries created a warm glow, engulfing the sea of faces before him. "The Freedom Celebration is a time to remember. In the beginning, it was simple. It was a time to stop and reflect on the King's protection and provision for us. We were in bondage. Ours was a physical bondage. We had become prisoners in a land we had called home for many years. Tonight, we remember the sacrifice that was required: a lamb, an innocent lamb. The blood of that sacrifice covered our doorways and protected us from death."

Yerde paused and looked toward Jael, "Those sacrifices are no longer required." Yerde's voice cracked, the garden was still. "Tonight, we also remember one who offered himself as a sacrifice. Blood was shed so that all who have yet to enter Turayn can be free from whatever bondage they find themselves. Tonight, we pause to reflect on the love of our King who was willing to offer such a sacrifice."

Yerde retrieved a piece of unleavened bread that lay on a plate in front of him. "In Turayn, the Freedom Celebration reminded us of our time held captive in a foreign land. It marked the events that led to our freedom. It was a feast to celebrate life, freedom, and the King's protection. Here in the Kingdom, partaking of this celebration. Here in the garden with Jael and our King, signifies the King's mercy and grace,

Jael's willingness to be the ultimate sacrifice, and our freedom from the bondage of fear and guilt. Let us eat."

As the group followed Yerde' instruction, each one reflected on their own memories. Those who had been in Turayn had so much to be thankful for. Those who had waited for family and friends to return to the Kingdom were consumed with excitement and anticipation. This celebration signified their King's willingness to forgive, his desire to make a way to bring them home.

The remainder of the evening was filled with food, drink, and reflective conversation. As the dinner came to an end, no one was eager to leave. There was a sweet peace that blanketed the garden. Each in attendance was filled with gratitude. As the celebration drew to a close, they all knew they had just experienced something divine.

"Thank you, my brother," Jael said as he turned to Konnory. "It could not have been more perfect."

"Thank you," Konnory said, "I see now why this meant so much to you. Next year in the Kingdom!" Konnory said as he raised his arm in celebration.

All echoed his cheer, "Next year in the Kingdom!" they all said in unison.

As the group slowly began to disperse, the King, Jael, Konnory, and Yerde returned to the head table and settled in. The attendants had replaced the evening's meal with the typical evening fare.

"I trust we have some Draught brewing in the kitchen," the King said as Tayten passed by.

"Yes, Sire. I expect it will be out here shortly."

"My friend," the King said, addressing Yerde, "wait till you taste this." Yerde couldn't help but smile at the King's expression of great anticipation.

"Thank you for accepting my invitation to be a part of tonight's celebration," Konnory said to Yerde.

"It was my pleasure," replied Yerde. "I shall never forget this night."

"There is another reason why I wanted you to join us," Konnory began. "I am continually perplexed by the humans' need to attempt to keep the Laws that Father gave them."

Yerde began to snicker, and then burst into a full-blown laugh. "They are what?" he asked. "They think they can keep the Laws? You mean they are actually trying to keep them?"

"They try miserably," offered Jael.

"Those who believe in the Laws use them more to condemn others. They are incapable of keeping them, but that doesn't stop them from pouring out guilt on those around them who are also unable to keep them," Konnory said.

"Next you'll tell me that they have made some order out of them, putting them from bad to worse," Yerde said. To his surprise, the group did not respond. "Are you serious? They have made an order out of them?" Konnory nodded. "Oh, so one law is worse than the other." Yerde thought for a moment. "I suppose the ten are the ones..." Yerde looked at the King "You recall that day, Sire?" The King nodded.

"You had rescued us, taken us out of our bondage. We were camped in a valley surrounded by Your protection. You called me up to that mountain."

Yerde paused, "We spent a great deal of time together. Several days, as a matter of fact. We talked about the arrogance that had entered those seeking forgiveness, that they were beginning to believe in their own abilities rather than your forgiveness. You told me of each Law. YOU had written them in stone with your own finger." Yerde looked around at the group, "That was something to behold. I was sitting, wedged into a crevasse of the mountain, covered from head to toe. You know those human bodies can only handle just so much." The group laughed.

"And if I recall," began the King, "You had your hands over your eyes the entire time."

"That's right, I did!" Yerde said. "I used them as added protection over my eyes, peeking through ever so tiny gaps between my fingers." Yerde demonstrated.

"When you finished, I picked up those stone tablets and made my journey back down the mountain. As I got closer to the camp, I could hear strange sounds. Not the quietness that typically covered the camp, this was as if there was a great celebration going on.

"As I rounded the last bend, the display that lay in front of me was evident. The entire camp was all gathered around what appeared to be a gold creature. My first reaction was surprise. How did they accomplish this? Then the heaviness of the stones brought my attention back to the King. A great anger overtook me. How could they? How could they have forgotten the King in such a short time? I was enraged. If I had the power to produce fireballs, I would have destroyed them all. All I had were the tablets that you had given me. Out of my anger, I threw them out into the crowd. As they hit the ground, they shattered. A hush spread across the camp. Most knew at that moment they had done wrong.

"As I stood, looking at those pieces of stone, my heart felt as if it had broken as well. I could do nothing more than make my way back up the mountain."

"It took you some time," said the King.

Yerde's head dropped. "Yes, I was in no hurry. Behind me was this group of people you had put in my charge, who apparently were unable to survive on their own, and ahead of me, was...you. How could I ever explain what had just happened?" Yerde looked at the King, "But you didn't need me to explain. You knew." Yerde smiled slightly, and the King nodded. "He then made me write them. Ten was all I could produce." Yerde sat quietly once again.

"They never truly understood. I knew when I did it, I would be opening the door to a long, long struggle. But at the time, it was the only choice. It was at a time when the Humans had become very arrogant. If there wasn't some miraculous sign to prove that I was with them, they would turn in an instant to follow Patho's beliefs. One minute they would be on their faces worshiping me and the next, they were drawing up plans for the next golden image they wanted to create. They needed to understand that they were incapable of forgiveness and returning to the Kingdom on their own. In fact, they needed to be reminded that they could not sustain life in Turayn without me.

"So I introduced a set of Laws. If you look at them closely, they are simply common sense. There is nothing in those Laws that doesn't make life better, safer, more desirable. There was one thread that linked them all together – keep all, if one were to be broken, they were all broken. It was impossible for the Humans to achieve. I knew that. That is why I instructed them back to sacrifice."

"It was shortly after," Yerde said, "that you gave us the instruction for the Temple. It was a magnificent place. Its order and beauty were the closest we had to the Kingdom."

"The Temple had one purpose, a place to give sacrifice. It was a visible reminder of the need for sacrifice," said the King.

"And that too they have distorted," said Jael.

"I didn't need all the rules and rituals," continued the King. "But they did. They needed a visual reminder."

"They still believe that they can keep all the Laws," Jael said. The King shook his head.

"They not only think they can do it, but that everyone else should keep them as well. They instill such fear in others." Konnory said.

"They believe they are good and right, even holy. They feel that somehow by striving to keep the Law they will gain my love...my protection...my blessing."

"They already have that," Konnory said.

"Of course, they do," the King replied. "But they don't know it. Turayn has become a place that is centered around achievements. It is such a struggle for them to think they can receive something without working for it..."

"When they have had it all the time," Konnory said, as he looked at Jael. "I'm not sure I would have done it," he said. "There are times they don't seem worth it."

"Don't forget, my friend," Jael said, "that deep within them is a soul, a Fallen Soul. That is why I did it. It's their exterior that gets in the way."

Tayten appeared at the end of the table. In his hands was the King's anxiously awaited Draught.

"Yes, it's here. Just wait till you taste this!" the King said as he clapped his hands together. Tayten poured a mug for each. Taking the first sip, the King said with great delight, "Perfect."

Konnory and Jael watched as Yerde took his first sip. As he brought the mug to his mouth, the steam filled his nostrils. "I've smelled this before," he said.

"Go on, try it," encouraged the King.

Yerde put the mug to his lips and slowly took in the first drops. He pulled the mug back and gazed down into it, "I've tasted this before...or at least something like it," he said.

"Yes, it was something similar, but it wasn't in a drink," Konnory said.

"No, it wasn't," Yerde said. He closed his eyes as he tried to remember. When he opened them, he opened them wide. He looked at the King, then to Konnory and Jael.

"Yes! He insisted on it," Konnory said, pointing to Father.

"We ate that every day, for years," Yerde said. "We never grew tired of it. Each day, morning and evening, we had anticipation and delight as we gathered it from the ground." Yerde took another sip. "I didn't realize how much I loved it until this moment."

Lost again in memory, Yerde began, "Each day, as part of your protection and provision, you sent nourishment to the camp, morning and evening. Each morning as we awoke, we would find a blanket of small pieces of what looked like bread covering the ground. We were instructed to collect only what was needed for the day. In the evening, the same happened. This went on for years. We called it manna from the Kingdom."

Finishing another sip of Draught, the King offered, "You are welcome to come anytime and join me. I am always looking for a reason for someone to brew a batch."

The King took another sip and Yerde joined him. He savored the taste. Looking down into the cup, he swirled it around. "Most did not understand the provision you had given to us," Yerde said.

"They still don't," Konnory said.

"The Law should have shown them how impossible it was, or is, to achieve forgiveness on their own," Yerde said.

"The Law still remains, but its purpose has changed. It's Patho's fear that has allowed it to become something feared."

"Sounds a bit like his confines," the King said.

"The idea of the Humans working so hard, striving for attention, striving for acceptance, when all they have to do is believe; It is Turayn's version of Patho's confines."

The group lingered well into the night. As the time drew near to end the evening, Yerde said his farewells and shared his gratitude for being invited to be a part of such an event. He gathered the family members that had accompanied him that night. Konnory and Jael watched as they exited the garden.

There was nothing in Yerde's demeanor that would indicate his life in Turayn. He had accomplished great things there. He had walked with the King and had known him as few others had. But the life lived in Turayn becomes unimportant when a Fallen Soul returns to the Kingdom. The moment a Fallen Souls enters the Kingdom, their life in Turayn becomes a blur. It simply becomes what it was meant to be - a way home.

20

Magnor and Quaine had worked side by side since they returned from their mission that had taken them to the Pit. Quaine was no longer limited to working with the Redeemed Warriors; Magnor involved him in every decision.

Waldemar had yet to visit the Stronghold. There was nothing inside of him that desired to venture out past the gardens. He had promised the King that he would escort the last of the Redeemed Warriors when they had completed their training. The King thought that perhaps Waldemar had extended this particular training in order to prolong the trip. But that day had finally come. The last Redeemed Warrior had successfully completed training and was scheduled to leave for the Stronghold in the morning.

The King noticed Waldemar's anxiety during dinner. As the meal came to an end and each began to take their leave, the King invited Waldemar to stay behind. As the two remained at the table and the attendants cleared the last of the serving pieces, the room quieted, and the King sat back in his seat. "Are you prepared for the morning?" he asked.

"Yes, I believe so," replied Waldemar. "The training is complete. It is always difficult to say goodbye and release them to join the ranks."

"As if you are sending a child away?" the King asked.

"As if I were sending a child away," Waldemar replied.

"Are you ready for your journey?" the King asked. Waldemar did not respond. "Have you changed your mind?"

"Given half the chance, I would," Waldemar admitted.

"What holds you back?" asked the King.

Waldemar sat quietly. He looked around the room; no one remained. The King waited patiently.

"When you and I walked in Turayn, it was more than I had ever hoped for. That day, the day you walked me out of Turayn and into the Kingdom...," Waldemar paused, his lips tightened as he tried to keep his composure, "...I was escorted home by the One whom I had walked away from." Waldemar looked down at his hands. He clenched them tightly. "There is nothing within me that wants to return to the Darkness. There is nothing that could draw me away."

The King smiled. He would never forget the moment he realized who Waldemar was. He remembered speaking those words, I do forgive. He recalled the day he led his trusted friend home. "No one is forcing you to go," the King said.

"I know. But I promised. I made a commitment to the Redeemed Warriors and I must keep my word. If I don't, what good is anything that I have told them?"

"You will gain strength from them," the King answered. "In going, you will find a new level of understanding. I say, you will find a new level of courage."

"I trust that is the case," Waldemar said, as he nervously rubbed his hands together. He looked around the room at the stillness of the evening. "I should go now. I must prepare for the morning."

The King watched as Waldemar walked through the doors. "You will find great strength tomorrow, my friend," the King said softly. "You will not return the same."

The next morning, the Queen escorted the King to meet Waldemar and his newest graduate. She could not help but notice the differences in the excitement of these two. The newly decorated warrior was eager to begin the journey. Waldemar seemed to be finding reasons to prolong it.

When all was finally prepared, the warrior turned and saluted the King. In response, the King held out his hand, and the warrior grasped it boldly.

"Congratulations, my son. We will all be waiting for the good report of your journey."

"Thank you, Sire. It is an honor to serve you in this way," the warrior beamed with pride.

"Waldemar," the Queen said, "send my love to my boys."

"I will give them the message," Waldemar replied. "Now we must be off." The two climbed in the chariot. Waldemar took the reins.

"Do you know how to drive this thing?" the King asked.

"He's the best we have," the warrior blurted out.

"That he is, that he is," said the King. Upon Waldemar's command, he and the small group that escorted him were off.

"I feel as if we just sent one of our sons off," said the Queen.

"Not a son, my love, a brother," replied the King.

"Ah yes, a dear, dear brother."

Quaine awaited Waldemar's arrival. He was eager to welcome him. He was excited to be able to spend time with him, and to visit the Redeemed Warriors who were currently standing guard in the Stronghold.

Magnor was also expected to return to the camp shortly. He had recently spent time with those guarding Turayn. There had yet to be a Redeemed Warrior assigned to Turayn. This was partially due to the apprehension of allowing them to be so far from the Kingdom. Mostly, it was due to the realization that they were stronger, more determined, and more resilient to the effects of being out in the Darkness. They were not as tempted as the others to interact with the Fallen Souls. They had an emotional stability that exceeded the other warriors when faced with standing guard and watching the struggle of the Fallen Souls. The Stronghold had great personal meaning for each of them. The Stronghold is where they desired to serve.

As Waldemar's small transport arrived, Quaine was there to greet them. "Finally, my friend, it is an honor to have you join us," he said, as Waldemar stepped out of the chariot.

"Thank you, my son," Waldemar replied. "Your mother sends her love."

"I'm surprised she isn't with you. Come, we have food prepared." Quaine led the group to a large tent.

They prepared their plates and took their seats at a table reserved for them. "After we give you time to rest from the journey, I will take you to the Stronghold. All the warriors are eager for your arrival. But the Redeemed Warriors are filled with great anticipation."

"When will I be able to join the ranks?" asked the newest warrior.

"Eager as all the others; I anticipated that," Quaine said.

"As soon as you are finished here, you will be taken to your camp to settle in. You will then observe the operations of the Stronghold. There is a viewing tower which stands inside the protection of the Kingdom which allows a full view. It's important that you see it from a distance before you become a part of it. Tonight, you will eat with the regiment that will serve as reinforcements. In the morning, you and the others will enter the Stronghold."

"Are you preparing to expand it?" asked the warrior.

"Yes, we are. This will be the fourth expansion we have done," replied Quaine. "The Watchers and Transporters continue to spread the word. The Fallen Souls are finding their way to safety."

Quaine directed his attention to Waldemar, "When Magnor arrives, the three of us will begin the inspection. Magnor will need time before we start out; it's something we have to force him to do. We take no chances; no one, not even he, is allowed to return to the Darkness without proper time in the Kingdom."

"I'm sure he thinks he is unstoppable," said Waldemar.

"You know him well," replied Quaine. The group continued eating with small chatter among them. The Redeemed Warrior finished first. Seeing the excitement and anxiety in him, Quaine excused him and sent him to his camp. "I love their eagerness when they arrive," he said. "What is even more amazing is that it continues to build, it never seems to fade away."

There was a confidence and contentment in Quaine's voice, a mannerism that Waldemar had not witnessed. It was contagious. As Waldemar observed, he too felt a new level of excitement for the days ahead.

"Might we make our way to the viewing tower before Magnor returns?" asked Waldemar.

"Of course!" Quaine replied.

The meal finished and those in attendance parted ways. Quaine led Waldemar to where he would be staying. Waldemar handed his belonging to the attendant, and then he and Quaine made their way to the viewing tower. As they began to climb the stairs, Waldemar recalled the times he had escorted the King in order to observe Jael in Turayn. This was going to be a very different view than that had been. He was not sure what to expect.

As they reached the top, Quaine directed Waldemar to the end. "You must remember, it is for their good," he said.

Waldemar walked slowly to the edge. He took a deep breath, raised his head and took his first look at the Stronghold. What he saw first was the wall of warriors. Strong, magnificent warriors, standing shoulder to shoulder to create a wall that stretched out into the Darkness. Seeing it for the first time made Waldemar's knees buckle. Quaine reached out to steady him.

"I know," Quaine said softly. "I know."

After gaining his strength, Waldemar forced himself to look at those within the Stronghold. If seeing the Darkness had unsteadied him, what effect would this have? He was surprised. As he looked out over the Fallen Souls, he was filled with confidence. There was a sense of expectation.

These who he had once been apart, were there awaiting their redemption. He suddenly found no reason to be terrified. Those outside the Stronghold, those were terrifying. But these, these had found their way to safety. For as long as needed, the King would provide for them a place to wait; a safe place. They did not have to fend for themselves any longer. They were protected – and he had the privilege to be a part of their protection.

"This is not what I had expected," he said boldly.

"Well, it doesn't seem as if it's too much for you to handle," replied Quaine.

"Why didn't I come sooner?" he asked. Quaine let out a joyous laugh.

"I am so very glad you have joined us!" Quaine replied, as he gave Waldemar an approving slap on the back.

The two remained on the tower. Quaine pointed out the Redeemed Warriors who were already a part of the Stronghold. They recalled stories of the beginning days of training when they both thought it would never be successful. Waldemar reminded Quaine of the day he offered to go with Magnor to the Pit. Waldemar confessed for the first time what a terrible idea he thought it was. "I thought you had finally lost your mind," he said.

"After it was all agreed upon, I thought I had as well," Quaine said.

Returning his attention to the Stronghold, he asked, "Where do they enter?"

"Originally, there was only one entrance. There - on the side," Quaine answered as he pointed.

"Yes, I see it," Waldemar said, as he followed Quaine's direction.

"But it was realized quickly that one was not sufficient. Since then, two more have been added."

Quaine pointed out the other entrances. Again, Waldemar followed Quaine's direction and observed the two additional entrances. Waldemar's head turned back toward the first entrance. He folded his arms and squinted a bit. He put one hand up to his chin, resting his head in his hand. Quaine observed him closely.

"Hmmm," Waldemar signed. He looked at Quaine and then back to his target.

"Are you going to let me in on what has your attention?" asked Quaine.

Waldemar stood a bit longer. Finally, he pointed toward the entrance. "Do we know who that is?"

"Who – who is?" Quaine responded, stepping to the rail for a closer look.

"That one – there – just outside the entrance," Waldemar pointed to a large figure standing yards away from the entrance.

"We don't know who any of them are. You know we can't do that. There is no conversation between us or them. It's much too dangerous," Quaine said.

"But why doesn't he go in?" Waldemar asked.

Now, Quaine was the one squinting and rubbing his chin. "Hmm," he sighed. The two stood watching. "I'm not sure,"

Quaine finally said. "Why are you so interested? What are you thinking?"

"How long have we been standing here? Quite a while, correct?" Quaine shrugged his shoulders. "He stands there watching. Several have walked by him and have made their entrance. He watches them enter, but he just stands there. Why doesn't he enter?"

Time passed as the two stood focused on the Fallen Soul. "We must find out what prevents him from entering," Waldemar finally responded.

"We can't force them," said Quaine.

"No, but...," Waldemar hesitated, "...there's something about him." Quaine's expression grew somber. They continued to watch.

The silence was broken by Magnor's greeting. "It's wonderful to see you," he said. His greeting made them both jump. "My word, what has your attention?"

Waldemar turned around and held out his hand in greeting. "Nothing," he answered. "We're just observing." Magnor looked at Quaine, who had an unexplainable expression.

"Are you going to share?" Magnor asked Quaine.

"Not today," Quaine replied. "If it's anything, we'll tell you tomorrow."

Magnor hesitated. "Well in that case, let's make our way back to the camp."

Quaine and Waldemar followed Magnor, but only after each had taken another look at the figure standing outside the gate.

That evening, final preparations were made for the following day. The newest Redeemed Warrior was briefed on what was expected of him. Quaine and Magnor escorted Waldemar though the camp. Waldemar was met with warm greetings from all the warriors. The following morning, Waldemar excused himself from breakfast before any of the others.

"Where are you off to?" Magnor asked.

"I would like to take one last look from the tower before we head out," Waldemar responded.

"I'll join you," offered Quaine.

"Don't think you're going alone. There is something out there, and you are going to tell me what it is," Magnor said in a very ordering tone. "I'll join you."

The three walked shoulder to shoulder and without realizing it, had the same stride. As they walked through the camp and toward the tower, they looked like one. They made it in record time and climbed the stairs without a word. As they approached the edge, Quaine and Waldemar stood motionless. "He's still there," Quaine said.

"Who's still where?" Magnor ordered.

Waldemar put his arm around Magnor's shoulder and directed his attention to the figure. "There, the one who stands at the entrance," Waldemar said softly.

"He was there yesterday," Quaine said.

Magnor looked out. He blinked. "He has been there longer than that," he said.

"What do you mean?" Quaine asked.

"I noticed him some time ago during an inspection. I had forgotten about it. But at the time it seemed odd," said Magnor.

"Do you think it is..." Quaine began. The three were silent.

"Whoever it is, there is a reason he stands and watches," said Waldemar.

"What do we do?" asked Quaine.

"We can't do anything," replied Magnor.

"We certainly can't bring him into the Kingdom," Quaine said softly. There was silence once again.

"Excuse me, Sir," said a voice from the stairs, which startled the three onlookers. "I'm sorry to disturb you, but the troops are waiting,"

"Yes, tell them we are on our way," Magnor said. The excitement of the day mingled with the reluctance to leave the tower.

Magnor, Quaine, and Waldemar spent the day greeting and interacting with the warriors who made the outer wall of the Stronghold. They were in preparation to once again increase their boundaries. Replacement warriors were put in place; the expansion was scheduled for the following day. The three did their best to give the warriors their undivided attention. But all were plagued with the image of the figure that stood outside the entrance.

That night as they sat around the fire, their conversation remained limited. No one spoke the words, but each could not help but wonder if this one, this one who stood outside the protection of the King, was Palti.

"You can't bring him home as you did me," Quaine said.

"First of all, there are no trees." Quaine always knew how to break the heaviness.

"We could send a Transporter out to speak with him," offered Waldemar.

"We can!" Magnor said as he jumped out of his chair. He began to call out orders, and within minutes a Transporter was standing in their presence.

"What do you have for me?" the Transporter asked.

"There is a figure who stands outside the entrance. He watches as other pass by him, yet, he never enters. He has been there for some time." Magnor replied.

"Yes, he has. We have noticed him," replied the Transporter.

"We want to find out why. Tomorrow, we would like for you to interact with him. See if he will offer you any insight," Waldemar said.

"Certainly," the Transporter said.

The next morning the curious trio left their tents before anyone else stirred. They made their way to the tower. Again the three stood and watched in anticipation.

"There, there he is."

"He doesn't move."

"What is he up to?"

"Why doesn't he enter?"

Eventually, the Transporter came on the scene. Magnor was the first to see him. He pointed him out. They watched. The Transporter made his way from the Kingdom to the entrance and cautiously approached the figure. The three stood motionless. There was a unified sigh of relief when they realized the two were interacting. The discussion lasted a while and the three observers wanted desperately to know what was being said.

A short time later, the Transporter began to move, and the figure followed. "He's taking him to another entrance," Quaine said.

They watched as the two passed the second and then the third entrance. They watched as the two stopped and continued their discussion. They sighed as the figure turned and walked away.

"What is he doing?" Magnor asked with desperation in his voice.

"Calm yourself," Waldemar ordered. "You can't fix this one."

They stood, helplessly watching as the separation between the figure and the Transporter grew. It wasn't long before the large, dark figure blended into the Darkness.

When the Transporter entered the Kingdom, the three turned in unison and ran for the stairs. Magnor led the way; he skipped every other step in order to get down quicker.

Quaine held on to the railings and seemed to touch every fourth step. Waldemar was right behind them. They darted for Magnor's tent. They were half running yet trying not to draw attention. It didn't work. They drew the attention of everyone they passed. Most were unsure what to think. When two Princes and a commanding officer who once was the King's second in command go running past, something must have been happening. The three made it back to their tent, leaving a path of confused and concerned warriors behind.

Within minutes, the Transporter was at the door. "Come in, come in. Take a seat. Did you find him?" Quaine asked.

The other two looked at Quaine in confusion. Of course, he found him, we witnessed it, they both thought.

"Yes, I believe I did."

"AND...." It was taking all of Magnor's strength to stay in control.

"He seems to have a purpose, but it's confusing to me. He said he wanted to understand the workings of the Stronghold."

"Does he want to enter?" asked Quaine.

"No, that is not his intent, at least not now," the Transporter replied.

"Is he planning some type of an attack?" asked Waldemar.

"No," the Transporter said hesitantly. "Well, not an attack on the King's Stronghold."

"There is another one?" Waldemar asked.

As the words left his lips, Quaine and Magnor locked eyes. There was another! They had seen it! It wasn't anything like the King's Stronghold, but there was most certainly another.

There was a long pause. They all wanted to ask but were afraid of the answer. "Did he give you his name?" Quaine asked.

"He did. He was reluctant to offer it, but eventually he did. He said he was part of a large group, a group that had been freed from Patho's control. He was not sure how many still remained in the Darkness, but he felt certain it was enough to form an army. He claimed he wasn't part of Patho's Departure, that he had left the Kingdom prior."

Magnor's jaw dropped. Quaine's eyes widened. Waldemar whispered, "The Others."

"Yes," the Transporter replied, pointing to Waldemar, "he used that word - Others. He also referred to the Multitude. I couldn't tell if he was referring to those bound in Patho's confines or if he meant another group," said the Transporter. He had done his best to make sense of their conversation, but to no avail. After all, it wasn't his job to understand. His job was to deliver the message.

"Thank you," Magnor said as he dismissed the Transporter.

"My pleasure," he said as he turned and left the tent.

These three brave warriors just stood there, motionless. "Jael freed the Multitude while in Turayn," Quaine said. "I was present when he did it."

"Two captains had informed Father that they had received requests from a large group of souls who claimed to be Others," Magnor said.

"No?" asked Quaine. "Are you serious? They had asked to be sent into animals on the hillside. When Jael gave them permission, they did, and the animals fled into the water and drowned. I thought that was what they meant. You mean they returned to the Darkness?"

"Apparently," replied Magnor. "The commanders brought their request to Father because it was confusing. Carasi said he thought it would work. As far as I know, we are unaware of any of them returning to the Kingdom."

"Returning to the Kingdom?" questioned Quaine, "I'm still trying to understand how they returned to the Darkness."

"Does it really matter?" asked Waldemar. "That has little to do with the fact that they are planning something."

"Are they planning to overtake...?" Quaine asked. "You don't think..." Quaine's questioning turned to realization and a fire began to burn in him.

Magnor rolled his head backwards. With a loud clap of his hands over his head he proclaimed, "Oh, His Ugly Highest isn't going to like this."

"Is it possible?" Waldemar asked, with the slightest hint of laughter in his voice. "Is the Multitude planning an attack to free those Patho is holding captive? What would such an attack even look like?"

"It's very possible," said Quaine. "From what we observed, it won't take much to destroy Patho's chain of missing links."

"Chain of missing links! That's hilarious!" Magnor said. What had been a very weighted discussion just a few moments ago was now bringing them great satisfaction.

"What's so funny?" asked a voice at the door. They turned in unison, knowing exactly who was there.

"Father, it's so good to see you," Quaine said.

"I understand we have some new developments," said the King.

Magnor and Quaine looked at each other. Each had a boyish look that echoed how did he know?

Waldemar smiled and shook his head. "What took you so long?" he asked.

21

Abaddon entered the Pit in his usual disgust, "Have you seen those three?"

"Who?" snapped Secretary from his crouched position behind his desk.

"Sul, Syrus, and that other one," Abaddon said from the doorway.

"As little as possible," answered Secretary, not bothering to look up. "Are they supposed to be here? I have no record of a meeting."

"They were to meet me..."

"I don't keep your schedule," Secretary snarled.

"I'm heading out back," said Abaddon.

"There are no problems, right?" asked Secretary, still engrossed in his work and taking no effort to address Abaddon directly. This did not in any way bother Abaddon. He had seen much too much of the Pit, Secretary, Patho, and Serpent. That was when Serpent felt it necessary to be present. All Abaddon wanted to do was return to his full-time duties in Turayn. He assumed that his return to former duties would only be possible when the Pit's confine was operating according to Patho's satisfaction. Unfortunately, he had never known Patho to be satisfied.

Abaddon turned to exit when he ran directly into Syrus, who was standing behind and much too close. "Out of my way," Abaddon said as he shoved him off. Syrus backed up to the doorpost, causing Sam and Sul to bump up against the wall. Abaddon walked out the door, and after steadying themselves, the three followed.

"You're late," said Abaddon.

"We thought we were meeting out back," offered Sam.

"It isn't your place to think," said Abaddon. "It's your job to obey."

The Pit was surprisingly large from the outside, much larger than it felt on the inside. Abaddon always felt that it should take a much shorter time to get to the back of the Pit than it actually did.

As the four drew closer to the end of the Pit, they began to hear the sounds of those being held within its confines. As they cleared the Pit and turned slightly, the confines became visible. Unlike the warriors who had accompanied Magnor and Quaine, they offered little reaction. These four had seen the plans from the beginning; they were there when the forged chains were delivered. They had found the volunteers who had agreed to hold the Fallen Souls captive. Besides, pity, compassion, or concern were emotions they had made unavailable.

"The fools," Abaddon, said looking out over the confines. Sam, Syrus, and Sul let out disgusting chuckles.

"Volunteers?" Abaddon asked, not turning his attention.

"For what?" replied Sul.

Syrus reached out and slugged him. "He's not asking if you want to volunteer," he said. "We have sufficient for our current needs and a large supply waiting their turn."

"What's changed, why so many now?" asked Abaddon. Abaddon rarely addressed the three directly and this was no different, he had yet to look at them.

"We have a new strategy," answered Sam. "As soon as we are aware that an FS has returned, they are greeted by...,"

"An FS?" Abaddon interrupted. "What the ... oh, I see...a Fallen..."

"Soul," Sam said. "They are greeted by a squadron who attack immediately. They convince the FS that their return to the Darkness is the King's fault. We have found that the closer the attack comes to the time of their return, the quicker and easier it is for them to be convinced. Once convinced, they are ours."

"A very solid plan," offered Abaddon. "It's similar to what we use in Turayn. It is essential to attack the human as soon as an unexpected event happens, in order to instill hatred and resentment toward the King. It's been very successful there; I would imagine the same would be true here."

There was a brief pause as they surveyed the confines. "Has there been anyone who has attempted to escape?" Abaddon asked.

"No," replied Syrus.

"Are you sure?" asked Abaddon.

"Yes, sire, quite," answered Syrus with a hideous laugh.

"Why so certain?" asked Abaddon.

"Because," Syrus continued, "if one would make such an attempt, they would most certainly succeed. There is nothing holding them here but their own fears. If one were to get the notion to escape, all that would be required is to simply step over the chain. It is likely that many would follow and we would lose control."

"Fools," Abaddon said in a very Patho like tone. "How are you ensuring that Pit Fear continues to be instilled?

"That's the best," Sam said with great enthusiasm. "Those holding the chains are rehearsed in a multitude of refutations. They continually instill in the FS Pit Fear and the suggestion that there is no means of escape. As long as we keep them at a particular level of self-condemnation and fear of the unknown, they remain and will remain."

"Self-condemnation and fear of the unknown; you did learn something in Turayn after all," Abaddon said. "That's what all the Pathonians serving in Turayn are trained to use. It is the simplest and fasted way to crush their spirit and hopes, and is very useful in creating a wedge between them and the King. Interestingly, it has greater impact on those who have the most to offer." Abaddon stood for a moment, "I ache to be back in Turayn," he said under his breath.

It was no wonder the sight of Patho's confines had had such an effect on the warriors. Those standing around its perimeter were not strong, but rather weak and insignificant figures; each holding one or two links of a single iron chain. At some points, the chain actually fell so low that it could easily be stepped over with very little effort.

Inside this perimeter is what had truly affected the warriors; for inside this weak and seemingly pointless perimeter, were Fallen Souls who had been so filled with fear of the unknown, that we had become prisoners of their own fears. With moans of anguish and screams of terror, these imprisoned Fallen Souls were being held captive by their own choosing. Unlike the warriors, these four observers had no emotional ties. For them, it was a sign of a successful mission and had become entertaining as well as empowering. To think that such force could be executed with so little effort, and so little manpower. For them, there was no equal for Pit Fear. It was their strongest and most successful line of defense.

"I don't need to see anymore," Abaddon said as he turned back toward the Pit. "We're done here." The three began to disperse when Abaddon abruptly blurted out, "Who's that?"

They turned instantly. Following Abaddon's direction, they sighted a large dark figure standing beyond the confines.

"Don't bother with him," Syrus said.

"It's best to leave him alone," said Sam.

"Why? What's his story?" asked Abaddon.

"We aren't sure, but he is not one to be reckoned with," answered Syrus. "We've attempted to approach him a few times, but he'll have nothing to do with us."

"Serpent says he is not an FS and we should not bother with him," offered Sul. "There is something very odd about him. Even his appearance is different."

"He's an Other," Abaddon said, partially asking, but mostly stating.

"That's what we thought at first, but ..." began Sul.

"But what?" demanded Abaddon.

"He is just an odd fellow," offered Sul.

"Is he alone?" asked Abaddon. There was no response. "You don't know?" Abaddon waited for an answer.

"We aren't sure," replied Syrus. "We think he is alone, but nothing about him is typical of anyone else we've come in contact with."

"Does he just stand there and watch?" asked Abaddon.

"Most of the time. He will disappear for a time, but always returns," said Syrus.

"Where does he go?" asked Abaddon.

"We don't know," said Sam.

"It's your job to know," said Abaddon. "Any one, or thing, that cannot be controlled or even swayed by Pit Fear should be... feared. Watch him closely. We need to get Serpent on him."

"I don't think Serpent will have anything to do with him," offered Sul

After the slightest pause, Abaddon shouted, "GO, WE ARE DONE!" The three tripped over themselves in an attempt to follow Abaddon's instructions. "Fools," Abaddon said, as he turned to make his way back to the Pit.

Abaddon informed Secretary that he would be gone for a time, that he would inform the Pit when he returned, and that he was in need of no one's assistance. Secretary considered the instructions as insignificant and continued with his work.

Abaddon left the Pit and headed toward the Kingdom. He had not made this trip for a very long time, not since the early days of Turayn. He had most recently felt trapped in the Pit, rarely making trips to Turayn. After observing the Pit's confines, he thought it would be important for him to finally see the King's Stronghold. He could only imagine how presumptuous it must be. After all, the King had no chance in redeeming everyone. Even with the Stronghold, Abaddon knew that once in Turayn, the Fallen Souls were fair game. He had his own army that was skilled in destroying any attempted relationship the Humans thought they could have with the King. Abaddon made his way through the Darkness, endeavoring not to interact with any Fallen Souls he passed along the way.

As Abaddon grew closer, the light radiating from the Kingdom began to part the darkness. Abaddon held his hand up to block it. He had forgotten the brilliance of the Kingdom. Knowing that the Stronghold was on the opposite side of Turayn, Abaddon veered slightly in hopes he would discover it soon.

He was slowly becoming acclimated to the light from the Kingdom, but it was not an experience he wanted to continue for any longer than was absolutely necessary. Patho's confines could be heard a great distance away. Surely there would be noises coming from the King's Stronghold.

The light began to grow brighter. Abaddon covered himself once again in hopes of adjusting to it. Where were the screams? Why wasn't he able to hear?

As he slightly veered, he saw it. Even to him it was impressive. The light was blinding and it took all his effort not to close his eyes. There in the distance was a wall of warriors. He knew they were warriors. He was one of them once. They seem to tower over everyone. There wasn't a gap between them. From his vantage point, it was a wall of strength that seemed impregnable.

He pulled his garment over his head and tightened the rope around his waist. He kept his distance as he began to walk its parameter. In a short time, Abaddon realized that this was no small feat. The King's Stronghold made jest of Patho's confines. He stopped - realizing it would be a waste of time to attempt to walk around it. He stood and watched. There was a constant flow of Fallen Souls flowing through the entrance. Abaddon was not aware of the other two entrances also being flooded with those seeking protection. "Fools," he said softly.

"Are you calling them one, or are you in need of one," said an evil and recognizable voice from behind.

"Where did you come from?" Abaddon asked without turning.

"I come here frequently," replied Serpent.

"Why?"

"For entertainment," Serpent responded. The two snarled.

"A wall of warriors," said Abaddon, "Could he be any less creative?"

"Chains or warriors," said Serpent slowly, "I'll choossse chains any day." Serpent still remained slightly behind Abaddon. "I hear you were asking about our friend."

"Friend?" asked Abaddon, "Oh, yes, him. What do you know?"

"He's nothing really, but I would keep an eye on him if I were you," Serpent offered. "He's been here a long, long time."

"An Other?" Abaddon asked.

"It's more than that. He has had his run in with Patho. And I hear with Jael as well. Odd fellow – an odd fellow indeed."

"What do we do with him?" asked Abaddon.

"That'sss for you to decide," answered Serpent "You're no match for him. He has no use for Patho. Pit Fear doesn't work on him either. He does seem to enjoy watching the strongholdsss – both of them."

"Both of them?" asked Abaddon. "You've seen him here? By the Kingdom?"

"Indeed," replied Serpent.

"This doesn't interest you?" asked Abaddon.

"Why should it? Why would I start being interested in him? I have no interest in anyone. I have no use for him or him for me. I'm done with you." And in an instant, he was gone.

Abaddon remained a short time longer. When he had seen enough, he turned to make his way back to the Pit. "Warriors – imbeciles of the Kingdom," he mumbled. "They will never overpower us. They are the King's puppets."

Abaddon tightened his garment around him. He pulled his hood as far over his face as possible. As he passed the Kingdom, he made one unexpected detour, "I'll be in Turayn," he said, as if giving direction. "Patho can find me, if he needs me."

22

Jael, Konnory, and the Queen were the only ones in the Dining Room for breakfast. As the three took their seats, Ferrul and Carasi burst into the room.

"Mother, we need to..." Carasi said.

"Go!" Mother said, "There is no time to waste."

"We need you two as well," Ferrul said, pointing to Jael and Konnory, catching them by surprise. After a reassuring look from Mother, the two pushed their chairs back and stood. Ferrul and Carasi led the way with Jael and Konnory close behind.

"Do you have any idea what we're doing?" Konnory asked Jael.

"Not a clue, but I'm guessing neither of us wants to miss it," Jael responded.

The four were heading for the front gates of the castle where they found their chariots waiting for them. Ferrul and Carasi boarded the first, and Jael and Konnory entered the second. Within moments, they were off. They sped through the Kingdom, heading toward the camps. When they arrived, they were greeted by Magnor.

"Glad you were able to come so quickly," Magnor said. "Father wants each of us to be a part, he was insistent that none of us be excused."

The four brothers exited their chariots and followed Magnor to the King's tent. Quaine was there to greet them. "Father has given final instructions, now we wait," he said as he greeted each brother.

"I trust there will be time to fill us in?" Konnory asked.

"Feeling a bit lost?" Ferrul asked.

"A bit, but we are used to it when you two are in charge," Konnory jested.

"Let's take them to the viewing tower. I'll send word to have Father meet us there," Quaine said.

As the six brothers made their way to the tower, they turned heads. It was a rare occasion to have all six together, especially out in the camps with the warriors. The sense of excitement and anticipation spread through the camp. No one knew for sure what was about to happen, but each knew there was something on the horizon. Father and Waldemar met them at the steps of the tower. Father had a joyous expression, which eliminated any concern either Jael or Konnory may have been holding on to.

"Welcome, sons," He said as he greeted each one. Holding his arm as to direct them up the steps, Magnor led the way.

It wasn't until Magnor reached the top step that he realized neither Konnory nor Jael had been here. Neither had seen the Stronghold. "Wait!" he shouted as he turned around and held out his hand to stop them.

"What? What's the matter?" asked Quaine with great concern.

"These two have not been here before," Magnor replied.

"Your right!" said Quaine.

"Oh," said Waldemar. "How did we miss that?"

"I'm sure it's nothing we can't handle," Konnory answered.

"It's not that you can't handle it," Quaine said, "It's how much you handle it. The two of you now know the plight of the Fallen Souls, you are intimately acquainted with those in Turayn; what you are about to witness are those waiting for that opportunity. It's as if you've been following a treasure map for years and you are finally going to see the place where the treasures are hiding."

"Beautifully said, my son," Father said from the bottom of the steps.

"Please walk to the edge slowly," Magnor instructed. "You will have all the time you need to allow the scene to unfold before you."

Magnor moved to one side, and once reaching the top, Quaine moved opposite him. Ferrul and Carasi did the same. All watched expectantly as Jael and Konnory took their final step and began to walk to the edge. Konnory was beaming. He closed his eyes, taking it in. Jael stood motionless. Konnory put his arm around Jael's shoulders. "They are going to make it," he said gently. "They are going to make the journey."

Jael couldn't speak. His eyes began to well up. He bit his lip. Father was now standing behind them. He placed his large strong hands on each of their shoulders. He squeezed them both gently. "Yes, they are going to make the journey," he said.

No one moved. No one had any need of making this moment move along quickly. Each had their own experience of seeing the Fallen Souls who had come to the Stronghold for protection. The strength of the warrior contrasted the weakness of the Fallen Souls, all surrounded by the vast Darkness. They waited patiently.

It was Father who eventually broke the silence. "Do you see that figure standing just outside the entrance?" he asked.

Magnor pointed him out. "He has become an interesting player. Jael, I believe you know him."

"Father, you don't mean to say it's..." Konnory blurted out.

"No, it isn't Palti," the King said in a very reassuring tone. "He is someone who has decided to take on Patho in an attempt to destroy Patho's confines." Being the first time either Jael or Konnory had heard of recent events, they looked at each other, surprised and intrigued.

"Why do you believe I know him?" Jael asked.

"Do you recall the Multitude?" Father asked.

"The Multitude," Jael whispered. He began nodding his head.

"Yes, the Multitude – in Turayn. The ones who asked to be set free?"

"Yes, those," Quaine replied in acknowledgment. Jael looked at Quaine. "Yes, I was there."

"You were, weren't you?" Jael asked. "We watched them enter the livestock. We watched as they fled into the water."

"He is their leader. He is the one that asked that you allow them to be set free," Father said.

Jael leapt off the ground and punched the air with his fist. The others began to laugh. "Yes!" Jael shouted. "Show them what it is to be FREE!!!"

Magnor, Carasi, and Ferrul began to applaud. Konnory stretch out his arms toward the figure and began bowing.

Quaine shouted "YES!", and Waldemar began to tear up.

An unexplainable chill went through Patho when Jael said these words. He wasn't sure why, but it was very similar to the feeling he had when the light began to glow just before Jael walked out of the Pit. Patho began to shout, "Abaddon! Where's Abaddon?"

Secretary slowly stood from his crouched position. He shuffled toward Patho's door and looked in, "You need something?"

"Abaddon! Where is he?"

"Couldn't tell you, haven't seen him for some time," responded Secretary.

"You had better find him and find him fast or YOU won't be seen for some time," Patho ordered. "Something is, or has happened. I can sense it. Send out word – we need to know if anyone has details."

"Details about what?" asked Secretary. "About something you think has or is happening. Good luck with that."

Patho's nostrils began to heave. He squinted his eyes. By now he was twitching uncontrollably. "GET ME ABADDON - AND SERPENT - AND GET THEM NOW!"

Secretary turned and began sending out orders. He was moving a bit faster, but not nearly fast enough for Patho. "Perhaps your plan of offering Abaddon forgiveness worked after all," he said softly.

Those in the tower watched as a Messenger approached the one they now called Leader.

"What's happening?" asked Jael.

"Father has given the Messenger instructions to be delivered to Leader," replied Magnor.

"I could not tell them what to do; I could only offer instruction on planning their attempt. We cannot have a battle in the Darkness. And besides, this is not a battle to be fought with swords and weapons. This is a battle to be won with thought."

They watched as the Messenger finished giving the King's instructions. He then turned and pointed toward the tower. When Leader caught sight of the King, he saluted, and then put his hand over his heart. With that, he turned and disappeared into the Darkness.

"Now what?" asked Konnory.

"Now we wait," instructed the King.

"But we cannot afford to wait together," instructed Carasi. "Jael and Konnory, you will need to return to Turayn and stay with the warriors. If for any reason this doesn't go as expected, Jael you still hold the power to end it. If at any time, there is any concern that Turayn is in danger and we are unable to continue, you will give orders from there."

"Magnor and Quaine have already organized troops here and will react according to Father's instruction. We do not know how long this will take, so be prepared," Ferrul said.

"We have no time to spare," Carasi said. He was already becoming annoyed that no one had begun toward the stairs, "we must move!"

With that, the small group made their way down the stairs. At the bottom, Jael turned to Father and asked, "What were your instructions?"

"I simply said, this was not a battle to be fought on the ground. It is a battle that must be fought from the mind. Patho's only defense is fear – it is fear that must be overcome."

The group disbanded. Jael and Konnory were surrounded by Watchers as they left for Turayn to meet the warriors. Magnor and Quaine headed off to be with the troops. Carasi and Ferrul were escorted to the communication tent. The King and Waldemar walked back up the stairs of the tower.

"Will it be successful?" asked Waldemar.

The King had been asked this very question before. It was long before Waldemar had returned home, long before Jael had entered Turayn as a Human. It was just after The Plan had been drawn up and was waiting its start. An unexpected servant had entered the Dining Room one evening and noticing the King's uneasiness, had spoken those same words. "Will it be successful?" The King recalled it as if it were yesterday. He recalled his hesitant answer as well, "Let us hope so my friend, let us hope so."

Waldemar could not help but notice the change in the King's expression. It was the same expression he had when they returned from a successful battle many lifetimes ago. "Yes, my friend, it will be," was his reply.

The Pit was once again in a state of upheaval. Patho had everyone on guard, but no one knew why.

Sul, Syrus, and Sam were heading toward the confines to enforce those standing guard. Serpent had been summoned, but had not shown up, and there was still no word from Abaddon.

The Leader of the Multitude had returned to Patho's confines. He had gathered many of the Others who Patho had bound together with him, and they were standing on the outside of the chain. Sul, Syrus, and Sam noticed, but were to preoccupied to do anything about it. It didn't seem as if they were a threat. Serpent finally made an appearance. After enduring Patho's rant, Patho ordered him to see what was happening at the confines, but he refused, and settled into his favorite corner of the Pit to watch the show. Unable to stand the suspense any longer, Patho decided he needed to make a personal appearance. He ordered Secretary to join him; reluctantly he did. This was quite enough to change Serpent's mind. The developments outside the Pit were proving to be more interesting than those he was currently observing.

As the three exited the Pit and slithered their way to the confines, word was sent to Sul, Syrus, and Sam to expect their arrival. The news was met with a new level of anxiety. They were too distracted to notice that the Multitude had entered the confines.

As Patho, Secretary, and Serpent turned the corner, they were greeted by Sul, who escorted them to where he felt was the best vantage point. Syrus and Sam were waiting for them there. The six stood in silence.

Eventually Syrus began, "We've been watching that figure right over there for some time."

"Over where?" Secretary asked.

Syrus began to focus in on where he had last seen The Leader. Sam and Sul joined him. Beads of anxiety formed on their brows. Sam began to twitch and Sul's arm trembled. "He always stands...right there...?"

Serpent hissed. "Do you mean him?" Serpent nodded toward the confines. "The one moving to the center of the confines?"

"When? How?" Sul was stammering terribly.

The six stood fixated on the figure now standing dead center of the confines. Sam and Sul were trembling, Syrus began rocking back and forth, and Patho was twitching uncontrollably. They were unable to speak, fearful of what they might be witnessing. The Leader of the Multitude stopped. Looking down upon a Fallen Soul, he reached out and took one's hand. The Fallen Soul looked up into his face. This one who had not felt anything but torment and excoriating fear, suddenly calmed.

Leader looked at the soul standing on his other side and did the same. As the Fallen Soul felt his touch, he drew back, but Leader did not let him escape. He reached out once again and grabbed the hand. A calm began to consume him. The three stood for a few moments.

Those on the sidelines watched in disbelief. With a nod, Leader instructed the two whose hands he held, to reach for the hand of one close to them. With a hint of reluctance, they did. As the Fallen Souls locked eyes and held hands, the calmness grew. The reaction instantly became voluntary. Each Fallen Soul who was touched, in turn touched, and with each touch, calm entered Patho's confines and began to smother the Fear.

The Multitude that followed Leader into the confines watched, and with an approving nod, began doing the same. A new chain was being created within the confines. It began to spread and webbed its way around those imprisoned. Those observing were spellbound. With each connection, the web grew and strengthened. Patho began to groan with each breath.

With great determination, Leader took one step. The entire confines shifted. He took another...and then another...and another. The Fallen Souls now webbed together followed. Each step deliberate, each as if it were being calculated, each as if a warrior where marching toward the enemy.

Leader made his way to the edge of the confines. With each step forward, another trapped Fallen Soul grabbed hold, leaving no one behind. As they marched forward, Sam realized they were no longer holding hands, but were now locked arm in arm. Moving, stepping, marching toward freedom.

As Leader grew closer to the edge, Patho shouted "NO! STOP THEM!" Serpent hissed. Secretary allowed a burst of laughter to escape.

Sam, Syrus, and Sul watched in horror as Leader and this new army made its way to the edge. The three held their breath as they witnessed the Leader simply stepping over the chain and continuing on. Without hesitation, those linked together did the same. As each one stepped beyond the chain that once held them, a charge of energy was put forth. All the pain, anger, and fear was instantly being transformed and sent out into the universe as hope, faith, and redemption.

Those waiting in the camps felt each charge. Without needing to witness firsthand, they knew a battle was being fought and won.

Jael and Konnory could hardly contain themselves. As the energy crossed through the atmosphere, it magnified. By the time it reached the warriors surrounding Turayn, it was a power that could not be contained. Each warrior was engulfed in what felt like a blanket of strength. Jael and Konnory were unable to stand still. They were boys again, full of excitement over a victory. They began to jump and dance; this was a victory that required celebration.

Leader did not stop outside the confines, but instead, continued marching forward. With each step, this weak, pathetic army grew stronger. They marched until the Kingdom and King's Stronghold was in sight. Waldemar and the King saw them in the distance. They were a mutely crew. Dirty and ragged. Worn and exhausted. They were one of the most beautiful sights Waldemar or the King had ever seen.

"It's an army of unsuspecting warriors who have changed the future," Waldemar said.

"Indeed," said the King. "The tides have turned. It is the beginning of the end. Patho has lost his assumed control on every front. Those he intended to control have broken through. This will be a battle that will be remembered for eternity."

Leader continued marching forward. Each step echoing through the Darkness. He led the group to the entrance of the Stronghold. At the gate, he stopped, and with a gentle nod, acknowledged all those who had followed him to safety.

Each Fallen Soul was allowed to enter on their own strength, and by their own choice. Magnor and Quaine were prepared to extend the Stronghold and if need be, were prepared to extend it again. No one would be turned away. They didn't count how many entered that day; they did record that the boundaries were extended thrice to accommodate all that left Patho's hold.

As the last freed Fallen Soul entered the King's Stronghold, a Watcher approached Leader. The King observed as the two exchanged a few words. As the Watcher left, Leader stood with his head down, as the King watched from the tower.

He took a step toward the entrance and then stopped. He stood as if pondering his options. Taking a step backward, Leader looked up toward the viewing tower. He and the King were locked in each other's sight. He saluted. The King nodded, and then saluted back.

Leader stood gazing up. Slowly, the King began to wave him in, inviting him to enter. A soft smile came over his face. He began to shake his head gently. He placed his hand over his heart and patted his chest softly. Leader then pointed toward the Kingdom and mouthed, "I'll meet you in there." He saluted the King one last time, turned, and once again disappeared into the vast Darkness.

Waldemar wiped away a tear. The King took a deep breath, and in his all knowing way, confidently and quietly said, "Yes, my friend, I'll meet you in the Kingdom."

"Yes, my friend, I'll meet you in the Kingdom."

Other Titles from author Jeannie G Bruenning

The Plan Series:
      The Plan
      The Captive

The Memoirs of Beatrice Miller

Lessons Learned in Retail Managment

Define Your Purpose

Co-author of:
      Living Unstuck

Children's Books:
      Mr. Hobbin's Beautiful Things
      Your Waggon is a Saggin'

Stay connected at: www.jeanniebruenning.com

J. G. Bruenning

www.ingramcontent.com/pod-product-compliance
Lightning Source LLC
Chambersburg PA
CBHW021218250626
47155CB00008B/2862